EVERY DROP IS A MAN'S NIGHTMARE

EVERY DROP IS A MAN'S NIGHTMARE

STORIES

Megan Kamalei Kakimoto

BLOOMSBURY PUBLISHING
NEW YORK · LONDON · OXFORD · NEW DELHI · SYDNEY

BLOOMSBURY PUBLISHING
Bloomsbury Publishing Inc.
1385 Broadway, New York, NY 10018, USA

BLOOMSBURY, BLOOMSBURY PUBLISHING, and the Diana logo
are trademarks of Bloomsbury Publishing Plc

First published in the United States 2023

Copyright © Megan Kamalei Kakimoto, 2023

All rights reserved. No part of this publication may be reproduced or
transmitted in any form or by any means, electronic or mechanical,
including photocopying, recording, or any information storage or retrieval
system, without prior permission in writing from the publishers.

ISBN: HB: 978-1-63973-116-9; EBOOK: 978-1-63973-117-6

LIBRARY OF CONGRESS CATALOGING-IN-PUBLICATION DATA IS AVAILABLE

2 4 6 8 10 9 7 5 3 1

Typeset by Westchester Publishing Services
Printed and bound in the U.S.A.

To find out more about our authors and books visit
www.bloomsbury.com and sign up for our newsletters.

Bloomsbury books may be purchased for business or promotional use.
For information on bulk purchases please contact Macmillan Corporate
and Premium Sales Department at specialmarkets@macmillan.com.

For my parents

I remember thinking that once there had been a time when women died of brain fevers caught from the prick of their hat pins, and that still, after all this time, it was hard being a girl, lugging around these bodies that were never right—wounds that needed fixing, heads that needed hats, corrections, corrections.

—LORRIE MOORE, *WHO WILL RUN THE FROG HOSPITAL?*

CONTENTS

A Catalogue of Kānaka Superstitions, as Told by Your Mother	1
Every Drop Is a Man's Nightmare	4
Story of Men	40
Temporary Dwellers	53
Madwomen	72
Ms. Amelia's Salon for Women in Charge	102
Hotel Molokai	115
Aiko, the Writer	151
Some Things I Know About Elvis	183
Touch Me Like One of Your Island Girls: A Love Story	198
The Love and Decline of the Corpse Flower	230
Acknowledgments	*259*

A Catalogue of Kānaka Superstitions, as Told by Your Mother

Don't sleep with your feet by the door! Those dangling, dreaming toes are sweet as sucrose to the Night Marchers, and they will drag you from your slumber by your feet.

Don't sleep with your head under the open window! When the demon visits, he will wedge his knife through the slit and slice you open by the neck.

Don't drive over the Pali with pork in your car! The spirits of Kamapuaʻa and Pele will kindle a war in that tinderbox you call a head, leave you with the ashes of lifelong bad luck scattered over your mushy brain bits.

Don't saddle your boat with bananas! You'll flounder along the seas with more bad luck, and, of course, no more fish for you.

Don't smash the moʻo with your rubba slippa! That's our ʻaumakua. Every dead relative who hasn't passed over, confined to the wet elastic limbs of the house gecko. Could be cousin Jerry, he died last year. Or Molokaʻi grandma. Or your father.

Don't kill the moth! Could also be your father.

Don't give your sister a closed flower lei! She's hāpai, you know, due in just a few weeks, and if you close her womb like that, the baby will slip from her legs before it's ready, choking on its cord.

Don't bury those chopsticks in your rice! That's how we left the chopsticks at your dad's funeral, all straight up like that. Bad luck!

Don't whistle at night! You know what happens if the Night Marchers hear you? You know how fast they'll climb over the Koʻolaus just to whittle down your spirit? You'll have to put everything you've got into evading them should you hope to whistle and live. My baby honey girl, don't you want to live?

Don't stack those dishes like that! Four is a rotten number. You know the kanji for *shi* is the same kanji for death? How much money we've spent on your Japanese lessons, and still you make mistakes. You should study longer, work harder, learn our language, practice your penmanship, do good. Make your father proud. After everything that has happened to us, don't you want to make your father so proud?

Don't stand between your sister and her husband like that! You're not their kid, and anyway, you standing in the middle like that means you'll be the first to die. You like *make dead die*? What would I do without my baby? I can't live without you, my baby.

Don't pinch your nose like that! That smell is only fresh flowers, a flute of music in our house. No matter that we don't keep flowers here, the smell stay from the other side. The rush of plucked 'ilima, sweet pucker of puakenikeni, don't you know these are the fragrances of your father? His spirit is paying us a visit . . . finally.

Don't point at your father's headstone like that! His soul should be at peace, not summoned by the strength of your baby finger. You think he wants to be anywhere near this place? Leave him be, let him sleep.

Every Drop Is a Man's Nightmare

The first and only time she travels over the old Pali road with a container of pork, Sadie smears blood on the back seat of her parents' car. It's well past midnight, and the stretch of old Pali descends into darkness as they travel the bends of the mighty Koʻolaus. Sadie's stepfather, Lopaka, is behind the wheel; her mother, Kāhea, a skeletal squirm of a woman taking up space in the front seat. They are fleeing the rural shadows of Kaʻaʻawa for Pālolo, where they have a cottage and unkempt backyard and civilization to confront. Lightposts splash a weak gloss on the asphalt, and with only a few cars traveling the roads, Lopaka pressures the gas pedal, wedging himself into speed as a cat nestles in tight spaces.

Sadie has just gotten her period for the first time. She uses the hem of her new dress as a rag to sop the blood.

As they veer down the Pali, Lopaka rolls down the windows, gusts whistling old tunes through the old Nissan. Her mother's car, though Lopaka insists on driving. The wind flutters against the glass windows. Swaths of dark clouds migrate slowly over the ridgeline. The road steers around the Pali peaks, deprived of their pristine emerald sheen under the intensity of night. Sadie sees the seat drenched in the same darkness. She skims two fingers over the wet lip of her underwear and brings them to her nose, inhaling a whiff of blood so sharp she bares her head out the window.

I'm dying, she is convinced. *I'm going to die on the island's most haunted road, tearing over ancestor bones like they are nothing.*

Lopaka calls from the front seat, eyeing her horrified reflection in the rearview mirror: *Eh, whatchu doing back there, girl?*

The car rolls down the Nuʻuanu Pali tunnel that braids through the ridgeline, weak yellowed light blinking through the dark just long enough for Sadie to see the blotches that've soaked the back seat, a deep burgundy beetling through the otherwise gray nylon. *I'm bleeding*, she says, too quiet at first. The car rattles through the end of the tunnel, emerging onto the tree-lined highway. Lopaka says, *Say that again?* and Kāhea says, *Just let it go for now*, and Lopaka snaps back, *Girl needs for learn for speak up, no one can hear a damn thing she says*, and Sadie sniffs her hand and says to her mother, *I'm bleeding*. She leans forward, presenting her stained fingers. Kāhea glances at the blood, which by now has cemented into crimson arcing her cuticles. She looks at Sadie with a flash of remorse, and then she is grinning.

Oh, honey, it's about time. Sadie is twelve years old.

Sadie feels around her underwear, and they are tearing over potholes and poorly paved road, going 70, 75, 80, 82, when a small figure emerges, straddling the lane divider toward which the car is gunning, and Lopaka slams on the brakes. Their bodies hurtling into the seat belts, screeching. Someone is screaming. Steam skims the asphalt, choking the car's shell, the car is not moving, the person screeching stops screeching, goes quiet. They all go quiet. Sadie peers through the kicked-up dust, scans the dark road, spies a creature the size of a—a cat, maybe? Or perhaps an overweight mongoose, something that snips and snarls but to its core deeply fears you. She squints into the dark and sees a wild puaʻa hunched low to the ground, its bristly tail and charcoal snout accentuated by the car's high beams, which Lopaka flashes and flashes, and Kāhea whispers, *My god*, and then Sadie draws a breath at the sheen of blood she senses on its black coat. She stares at her fingers, sees the same blood.

Fucking rodent, Lopaka says, shifting the car back into drive and maneuvering around the wild boar bleeding or covered in blood or both. *Hunting season can't come soon enough.*

But Sadie would like nothing more than to rescue every single puaʻa, including the bleeding one, which she knows for certain her new stepfamily would ensnare instantly with their arcane muzzleloaders and hunting rifles. As the car propels forward, Sadie glances back at what she's just lost, a pua'a standing firm on its quarters, painted in ribbons of blooming burgundy, wagging its weedy tail like a pup that's been torn from its mother. She watches the pua'a until its outline bleeds into the stretch of haunted highway fading in their wake.

BY NOW SADIE has heard so many cautionary tales about the Pali that the warnings coat her tongue like paste. Because of this she thinks little of them, and maybe this is her first mistake.

Mostly the roots of the stories are knitted in antiquity, tales told by weary parents to ward off bad keiki behavior, bizarre legends the kūpuna cling to in some sad attempt to restore their withered culture. Whatever. Sadie's stepfather was never one to follow blind tradition; as for her mother, she is too blissed out on temporary love to regard anything or anyone besides her new husband. Though born Katherine, Sadie's mother immediately dropped the English like excess fat after she married Lopaka and now goes by Kāhea. Kāhea Kahananui, a great work embodied in human form, one who really couldn't give two shits about her island's origin stories.

But Lopaka's family, they believe in rotten luck. They believe in Night Marchers and Pele's wrath, in the sanctity of lava rock and the White Lady who hitchhikes her way through the city, testing the tensile goodness of men. They never whistle at night, and they sure as hell do not sleep with their prostrate toes pointing toward the bedroom door. To them, the grounds of the demolished Waiʻalae Drive-In still bear a likeness to the Faceless Ghost. They wake to a pressure in their chest and claim it's the work of the Choking Ghost, pressing up against their ribs.

Funny enough, then, is that it's Lopaka's family who hosts the dinner the night of the puaʻa sighting, the same family who packs the leftover pork in Tupperware and sends them on their way. The pork is a batch of kālua pig; Lopaka's father smokes it the traditional way, in a backyard imu dug by the family's four sons. Deep in the hills of Kaʻaʻawa, Sadie watches the spring of muscles flex and yield under her step-uncles' undershirts as they plunge their shovels into the dirt. She watches the burial of the carcass; then, eight hours later, its resurrection. Kiawe smoke plugs her nostrils, waters her eyes. When it comes time to hiala ʻai, she spoons a generous portion of salted pork over her plate, the oil wetting her fingers. Lopaka's family eats around the yard in intimate factions catalogued by age and gender, by ʻohana and the mere hānai. Sadie's mother eats on a plastic stool hunched over her food—scoops of white rice and lomi salmon, spoonfuls of soured poi the color of lavender and long rice and of course the very reason why they're there, Lopaka's favorite kālua pig. It is Lopaka's birthday, he is thirty-two years old. He eats at the termite-bitten picnic table near the garage, surrounded by his brothers and a few of their wives. The young cousins eat together, cross-legged and waist-deep in sprawling fountain grass. Sadie eats alone, her stomach curling in strange, aching ways. But the kālua pig tastes spectacular, and the more she eats, the better she feels.

When Sadie approaches the buffet table, all the brothers turn to examine her. Combing for seconds, of course. At this point they've come to expect it. Her step-uncles have grown fond of calling her the garbage disposal—she'll mop your food scraps clean, if you let her. This isn't the worst she's heard about her body.

Sadie considers what they see: a frumpy, chubby kine keiki with haole skin and a bowlegged waddle cloaked in cargo shorts. Sadie wraps her fingers reluctantly around the tongs, dishing a second helping of kālua pig onto her plate. *Sistah doesn't need seconds, she needs for run 'round the yard couple hundred times.* Her cheeks flush the bright red of a ripened Hayden mango; her mother pretends not to hear them. Lopaka's mother circles the buffet, slaps the son who spoke on the back of his buzzed neck. *Sistah can have all the kālua pig she likes, I going send her home with more than I going give you!* Tūtū holds Sadie's round face in her hands and says, *Eat as you please, honey girl.* But the uncle's words have already slaughtered her appetite.

So, the leftovers. If she refuses to eat a second helping, then she's responsible for the leftovers, and she doesn't want to be responsible for the leftovers, does she? Not if they're commuting over the Pali, because doesn't she know the legend? Hasn't Lopaka taught this native girl right? He's been in her life for over a year now, and shouldn't she know her own moʻolelo by now?

Just take the goddamn leftovers, Lopaka growls as they pack up to leave. *Not going make a difference.*

The moon is goddess Hina, arms outstretched to the inky spill of night.

My folks believe anything they can't understand, so long as the old aliʻi swear by it.

But Sadie hesitates to accept the Tupperware of kālua pig, so Lopaka makes the decision for her: he yanks the container from his mother's hands and ushers them to the car.

Good luck with that! One of the uncles calls from the garage, sweeping the floor of crumbs and mothballs, and when Sadie glances out the window, she sees a strange man running a single finger across his neck, grinning.

BACK HOME, SADIE reads up on blood. She scrolls through the internet and the old Hawaiian texts Lopaka has brought into their home, and then her mother sits her down on the toilet and shows her how to insert a tampon inside her. *Only got super plus*, she says, peeling the plastic wrapper quickly, like it's a candy bar. She hands Sadie the thing and it looks like the skin of a parachute someone's forgotten to deploy.

Sadie learns a lot that first night. She learns that blood and tissues are peeling from her uterine wall, and she learns this will happen once a month for the foreseeable future. She learns that she has two ovaries but only one uterus, the lining of which is soft and porous like a wet sponge. She learns the first period marks the start of puberty, which is a word that boys in her class spit with laughter, along with other words like *cunt*, *pubes*, *boobs*, *rack*, *69ing*, and *cumload*. She googles each one, finds her way back to menstruation every time.

She reads Lopaka's books, or tries to. There is only so much she can understand. She learns too much about her culture, things she wishes to unknow. She reads that in the high days of the aliʻi, wāhine ka wā haumia, or bleeding women, were regarded with a reverence otherwise reserved for royalty. They were kapu in a different way, a way that safeguarded their menstruation rather than debased it, so much so that the bleeding wāhine were isolated in the hale peʻa for the duration of their monthly period. The separation between men and women was enforced by a strict kapu—however long the menstruation lasted, the bleeding wāhine and their kāne were to exist in separate physical spaces. Anything less was shameful, pīlau, not because the women were indecent creatures, but rather because the women were gods.

Sitting in the swamp of her own menstrual blood, Sadie doesn't feel so much like a god as she does a bloodied fetus, some feral creature being unborn again and again.

YEARS LATER, AND Lopaka proves to be a good man hampered by a short temper. He turns over like a wet stone as thirty-two becomes thirty-five, forty-one, and then Sadie is twenty-one years old and enrolled in community college but still living in the basement of her parents' cottage. The home is nestled deep in Pālolo and is overrun with feral chickens; Sadie bikes six miles to campus three days a week. She and her mother take turns cooking dinner, a rotation of stews and baked chickens, hearty beef curries and roast pork slopped in savory brown gravy. All the while Lopaka spoils away in a peeling pleather recliner, pawnshop reality shows looping in the background. On the weekends, Sadie wrenches open the basement window and slips out into the night like a child evading her parents. She travels on foot, looking for Jason.

They met in an entry-level biology course, a subject foreign to them both and selected entirely for the ease of fulfilling a grad requirement. Sadie studies Hawaiian history; Jason, an aspiring accountant, fiddles with numbers like he's fashioning a new language. They peered at each other across the classroom, and during their second lab together, he approached her quickly and told her they should be partners. *Lab*, he clarified, and Sadie felt the fault lines in her chest rupture and split, carving a space for him.

Two weeks later, and Jason has taught her how to hold his penis firmly in her hands and rub out his most sensitive spots. From Jason she's learned to clench the muscles in her pelvis as if bracing for some terrible impact, and she's also learned men can be things other than cruel and tired. When they are not exchanging lab notes, Sadie and Jason are borrowing his father's pickup truck to drive the endless loops of Tantalus, where the tree tunnel wools their shadows in darkness. So dark, Sadie can reach across the stick shift to hold him in one fist and feel him grow.

Her stepfather: *That kānaka kid, ho, I like him.*

Her mother: *Sometimes they aren't always exactly who you think they are. You'll need to wait and see what kind of man he is.*

But Sadie needn't wait long. She tests him first by disrobing her fat body midday and scanning his face for smears of revulsion. Nothing sticks. Instead, he wraps his hands over her flop of breasts, pinches at the rolls that gather around her belly, kisses her anyway. Strange, really, for how long she's hurried past mirrors, terrified of her naked reflection, and for whatever reason Jason just can't get enough. It's silly and it's sad, but also terribly true the force with which she cries after he calls her beautiful and maybe she even believes him.

So one might understand that when Sadie gets her period for the first time in their union, she hides away. Feigns stomach cramps, a migraine, a bad batch of garlic shrimp from their lunch date at the campus café. For days, she refuses to see him. She loops herself in circles to mislead his impulse to fuck her. That month she bleeds through her super-absorbent tampons and the panty liners she tapes to her underwear, and when she squats over the toilet, she watches her own blood unfurl in clumped confetti that sinks to the bottom of the bowl and stains it.

He texts her, mostly late at night after she's gone to bed.

I miss you, can I bring you anything, soup, I can get you soup? I'd like to see you soon. Please get better. I can't stop thinking about you.

You drive me so crazy.

I think I might love you.

I'm so horny for you, baby, it's been so damn long.

Three days pass, and then her blood inhales like a vacuum back into the caverns of her body. The biting crimson softens to a requisite rust, and then one day she peels down her underwear and there is only the gummy film of her own desire bleeding into the fabric. She smiles. Shaves her legs and slips on her favorite olive dress with the bulky pockets and runs to Jason. She visits the apartment he shares with three other undergrads, beach bums with kind spirits who pass her on campus, say hi to her by name. Their two-bedroom unit is cramped and unfurnished, situated in the back of Kalihi Valley at the top of a sloped driveway. Two flat mattresses are parked in the 'Ewa corners of the bedrooms, bars line the jalousied windows like a jail cell, a ceiling fan pushes dust through the rooms. A cat with no name braids its body around the boys' many legs. When she visits, Jason immediately ushers her into the bathroom, where she sits on the lip of the mildewed tub and takes him promptly in her mouth because there's no time to waste.

He says, *I missed you so badly, baby.* He brushes the top of her head like he pets their nameless cat. She leans against the wall, swoons weary with love.

She returns home that night with semen smudged between her legs to an elaborate feast on display in the kitchen. Lopaka has decided to return to work repairing the Pali for the city, and so Kāhea celebrates by feeding the 'ohana until their bellies twinge with remorse. Pork is pleasure in their hale, which means the crunch of lechon kawali, kālua pig, homemade Spam musubi, and char siu pork are all on display. They pair the pork with the fluff of white rice steaming in the rice cooker, and somehow they do not argue but instead pinch crispy pork belly and stringy kālua pig between their chopsticks, not fighting. Sadie doesn't even bother to count the calories, saving the mathematical gymnastics for another meal entirely.

Lopaka will work the Pali this evening, the dreaded graveyard shift. For over half a century, the road's undergone significant trauma, its ancient kapu wrecked by speeding cars and pitted with potholes. It's as her tūtū says, *No one tells the old tales anymore.* In school, Sadie was taught basic biological principles and how to craft a persuasive essay. But there were no textbooks to tell the tale of Kamapuaʻa and Pele, of their torched love affair, and how lava coursed through his veins when Pele finally left him for good. How later Kamapuaʻa roamed the Pali for centuries on the soles of four bloodied trotters. How his ghostly presence curses those who dare to carry pork over the old Pali road. No, she learned the legend not from her kumu or her studies but in the gravelly tones of her tūtū's tales, and so of course she hasn't decided yet what to believe.

It is the most haunted road on the island, a two-lane highway where atrophied asphalt unfolds over the bones of dead ancestors, from makaʻāinana like her own late kūpuna to aliʻi as revered as Kalanikūpule himself. Descending from windward Oʻahu to the bustling hub of Honolulu, the road hooks around the contours of the Koʻolaus, and it is in this place of transition where things start to get interesting.

The stories vary depending on who is narrating. For some, the Pali is a channel of sanctity, where fire goddess Pelehonuamea holds in her heart a vengeful grudge against demigod Kamapuaʻa, her half-man, half-pig ex-lover. Take pork over the Pali and you'll find your car slowing under mysterious circumstances, the accelerator nothing more than an ornamental pedal on which to rest your foot.

For others, the stakes are so high as to be unspeakable. Dare to transport pork over the Pali and you'll face a lifetime's worth of rotten luck.

The guys was talking about the cursed Pali and its Night Marchers, trying for scare the new haoles on the crew, Lopaka says.

Kāhea shakes her head, clearing the table of her dish and the bowl that once held lechon, now a slick foil of grease marooned in its place. *You guys are a bunch of rascals*, she says.

Is it spooky on the Pali at night? Sadie asks.

No spookier than anywhere else on island. No tell tūtū that, though. Lopaka forages through a half-eaten bag of chicharrón, licking salt from his fingers. *She's like one walking book of ghost stories. But nothing bad ever went happen to her. Go figure.*

Sadie considers her tūtū, the tales she told and how she held Sadie's face between her hands like a delicate eggshell. The stiff kitchen chair presses against her pelvis, amplifying all the slop swimming in her cotton underwear, but it can't be—she just had her period, right? She leaves the table, bolts herself in the bathroom and tears the underwear from her thighs and sees blood. The downstairs bathroom in which she locks herself is mostly reserved for Lopaka and his midnight shits, so of course there are no tampons, no pads, no pantyliners, only the toilet paper she wraps around her palm like a sheath of gauze and roots into the liner, where blood globs the paper's flimsy surface.

Another pause, then. At least for now. Better to disengage from Jason for a while, better for them both.

She returns to the table, chews on a chicharrón, but it's the tarnish of blood Sadie tastes in the back of her throat.

BECAUSE THEY'RE STILL so young, they don't waste any time. Jason's blind optimism ushers them through a particularly difficult finals season, and then they are wading in the sludgy waters of Waikīkī Beach, Sadie scooping sand by the fistfuls while Jason fishes a ring from the zippered back pocket of his board shorts. He asks her to be his wife. It is an occupation voided of a frame, of hard edges and shadings, but what thrums low in her gut are vibrations of safety, and so how can she say no? So surprised, she hurls a fistful of sand at his face, and then she says, *Yes, of course, yes*, as he climbs up the shoreline, wipes his face with a towel.

They kiss ankle-deep in wet sand. Sure it could be any man with any ring, though Sadie is indeed grateful it is this man and this ring.

Her parents, too, are elated. Over the last few years, their savings account has deflated like the skin of a balloon, and Lopaka grows to resent the graveyard shift and the women inhabiting his home. They're running low on space and food, short on patience. The ring is a fake emerald gem studded with miniature diamond-like stones that glisten under the light; the band is too small and constricts her finger like a corset. When Sadie brings her engaged body into the house, Kāhea yanks on her ringed finger, brushes her thumb against the luminescent stones.

Never again must I impress another man, Sadie thinks, rubbing the stones. She lets her summer school studies slide and passes the season planning an intimate wedding to please no one but herself. To afford a moderate affair of sixty guests, Jason takes work on the Pali with her stepfather while Sadie buses tables for a mom-and-pop Hawaiian diner. She finds she excels at scrubbing dishes clean of lū'au leaves and poi stains, but Jason can't shovel gravel to save his life. Mediocrity leaks through his sweat, and when he brandishes a shovel he is reminded that, to his core, he is a feeble boy, not built for the work of his ancestors.

Eventually the excitement wears off, and the two slouch into the comfort of familiar routines. When Jason quits the construction gig, Sadie works double shifts at the restaurant to make up the lost income. The owners enjoy her company so much so they promote her to front of house, where she takes orders and jives with the customers, men with big-bellied laughs and construction vests who remind her of her step-uncles, her stepfather. She asks Jason to visit her at work someday, but he doesn't want to make the drive.

The wedding is now three months away, and Sadie has resolved to lose at least twenty pounds. Her dress is a soft ivory sheath with a plunging back and a dramatic lace chapel train that she sees behind her eyelids as she slumbers. But they won't be married in a chapel; it will be on the beach, blocks from where Jason proposed, and dirt will collect in the hem of her train as she pads barefoot through the sand. The dress hugs her pouch of belly like a clinging animal; no matter how fervently she runs, swims, the extra weight swirls around her.

So, no more pork. No more marbled slabs of beef or chicken thighs lathered in oil and fried with the skin on. No more sweets, and no more food that tastes good, because that goodness is only a drop on her tongue while the photos of Sadie in her dress will withstand time. During dinner with her family, Sadie skips over the pork chops slathered in gravy and brined from their own fat and the creamed corn and the white rice drenched in shoyu. She nibbles on raw vegetable sticks and rolls through the guest list in her head. She will look so goddamn good in her dress.

She's trying for make us feel bad, but I not going feel bad. Kāhea gestures toward her daughter, and Sadie swallows a mouthful of carrot that dissolves like dirt on her tongue.

She's trying to look perfect for the wedding, Jason says.

Always so worried about that kine stuff, Lopaka says. *You supposed to enjoy the wedding, eat plenny kine food, dance all night. You know how for enjoy, don't you?*

But Sadie doesn't know *how for enjoy*, not when men have passed judgments on the folds in her body and the revolting way her fat arms jostle when she walks. How can anyone expect a bride to know *how for enjoy* unless she resembles a skeleton of herself?

She stops eating meat, tells herself and others it's for the wedding entirely, and while this is true, there's something else, too, a hesitation that's walloped her since her very first period, when her parents dismissed the bleeding wild hog as nothing more than an inconvenience on their drive over the Pali. She feels as though time has suspended her in its invisible clutches, like her growth has been stunted since that evening drive. Something strange she left behind.

Later that night, they retire to Jason's apartment and Sadie lets him take her in any manner he pleases because she's sure his pleasure will be her own—what else is marriage than the infinity of a braided orgasm? When he runs a finger around the ring of her asshole, all she does is slip up with a low moan. Her stomach churns with hunger. He prods at her back and claws his fingers through her hair and after he comes he folds his head in the crook of her elbow and murmurs how beautiful she will look in that slinky white dress.

THE MORNING OF the ceremony, and Sadie wakes to blood webbed between her thighs and the tip of Jason's penis peeling sleep from her lips. He trembles above her, and she maneuvers in turn as though carving space for the rise of her chest. She wants to keep a piece of him close during the ceremony, so after he finishes, she slips into her dress and smears a wet wad of his cum on the hem of her flowing ivory train.

They marry the old-fashioned way. This is what their friends and family murmur among their standing factions while waiting for Sadie to walk down the aisle forged of sheared grass and plumeria petals. There are no seats draped in alabaster cloth, no minister poised at the front of a chapel, no bridesmaids or groomsmen or special recognition of the couple's parents amid the swell of orchestral melodies. Just a bunch of people standing around under the broiling summer heat while Sadie walks barefoot to greet her new husband. The officiant is Jason's roommate; his ordination license was emailed to him last week. Her bouquet, a simple collection of puakenikeni plucked from the flowering bushel in Lopaka's family home.

And that *dress*. Sadie's exceeded her goal, twenty-five pounds lost in just over three months, something magical.

She surveys the shock of the men as they work through what has happened to her body, and for a girl of her short stature, Sadie looms.

It was Jason's idea to marry near the beach where he proposed, which is why Sadie shuts up about the south swells that billow in from the sea, leaving the air tinged with saline and must. She says *I do* draped in a sticky film of sweat, and she pays no mind to the frantic myna birds' warbling in the swaying canopy of the monkeypod tree overhead, and beyond the tree, the chants and roars of a spikeball tournament rearing along the shore of Waikīkī Beach. She kisses him fully and feels his tongue like a fat stone in her mouth. When they reverse directions down the aisle, she is married. He whispers something in her ear, but all she hears are the haole tourists walking past and those damn myna birds.

What's that? she says.

Your dress, it's all stained. There's blood on your ass.

He recoils as though her body is mired in barbed wire.

She pivots and whirls, tugging at the lace hem of her gown, and it isn't until they've sprinted to the car parked along Monsarrat that Sadie is able to shield herself from the wandering tourists. She she crawls into the back seat and tugs the seam of her dress to find a mottled, fist-size patch the color of rust.

I'm bleeding, she says. She pokes the soft lumps of her inner thighs where the extra skin pushes through her underwear. While she bleeds, Jason weaves through Kalākaua Avenue, chauffeuring them to the wedding reception held in his family's Kāhala estate, where she will dance as a married woman, filling her belly with nothing but booze and good cheer, and she will bleed and feel something shift inside her, something without a name but with a vivid and terrible face.

From the driver's seat, Jason asks, *What's that, sweetheart?*

SLEEP DOESN'T COME, that first night. Nor does it come the second night, when Sadie bleeds so bad it soaks through the tampon and the bulk of her cotton underwear, imprinting their sheets with a deep vermillion stain the size of a toddler. Jason sleeps through the stirring but not through all her sounds, and when he asks her what's happened, her voice shreds to sobs.

It's true he comforts her. It's also true that on the second night of their marriage, Jason slips into a deep sleep on the living room sofa.

The problem is, since the morning of the ceremony, Sadie hasn't stopped bleeding. She unravels entire sleeves of toilet paper from the roll and sops up what she can, but by the first week in her new apartment shared among four grown men, Sadie has stained the toilet bowl in a dense ring of burgundy, and her cramps are intolerable, like they're sculpting her belly into something foreign, feral. No matter the weight she's lost and intends to keep off, because her appetite has all but withered to dust. From work she hauls home Styrofoam containers filled with tripe stew and squid lūʻau, lomi salmon and soggy pasteles and Jason's favorite pickled ogo, which he eats between mouthfuls of white rice drenched in chili pepper water, and don't the men just adore her. Sadie sits beside Jason in the kitchen, her fingers curled around his knee, sipping from a green smoothie she's likely to puke up late into the night.

Hawaiian food, she knows well, was curated by bellies of the aliʻi, not meant for women on diets.

She faints twice in the shower, and Jason is quick to lecture her on the benefits of eating more, bleeding less, as if either affords her the choice. When she loses consciousness a third time walking from her unit to the stairwell, Jason snatches back with fear. He lifts her like a laundry basket and helps her steady her way back home. The roommates make a big show of fussing over her, and then they leave for happy hour at Study Hall, where they recline under bamboo scaffolding woven in fake tropical vines, feeding on kālua pig tacos and cheap pitchers of Kirin. Back home, Sadie lies belly-down on the floor mattress; Jason kisses her forehead, walls their bodies apart with the plush of an old pillow.

Maybe it's time to see a doctor? he says, but Sadie refuses.

He folds over, doesn't know what to do with his arms or how to help her. *You could be anemic, iron deficient, you could need medication—can you imagine what would happen if you passed out while driving? While running? If I wasn't there . . .*

Sadie turns on her side to face him. *I don't want to see someone and have them tell me it's not going to get better. I'd rather not know than face that.*

Oh, honey, that's just silly. He pets her hair, traces his hand down to the bristly, sun-choked tips.

But Sadie is unconvinced. During her last visit to the doctor, a pediatrician with sinewy, gristled skin and old-man eyebrows, she not only was diagnosed as prediabetic, but she also endured nearly an hour of the old man lecturing her in his thick haole drawl on all the reasons why she was ripe for a diet. Her mother sat in the waiting room, staring at the face of her watch as though she could fast-forward time.

Now Sadie is skinny and beautiful and goddamnit she is *married*, and doesn't this mean she's no longer embroiled in the business of being beholden to men who are not her husband? Doesn't this tear the threads that once bound her as a single woman, now setting her free?

No, I don't want to see a doctor.

Jason retrieves the laptop on his desk and returns to the bed, where he begins sifting through the infinite Google scroll. She rolls back onto her belly and presses her face against the pillowcase, inhaling the smooth calm of lavender detergent while Jason interjects with his findings:

This article says vitamin C–rich foods help your body absorb iron. These include kiwis, red peppers, broccoli, strawberries, and brussels sprouts.

This one says to consume more foods that're high in iron, like oysters. Do you like oysters?

Did you know blackstrap molasses is a good source of iron?

Some people recommend a uterine artery embolization. Last resort, I guess.

She holds her face to the pillow and imagines what it would feel like to stop breathing altogether, how long Jason would talk to himself before realizing what's become of her. What has become of her?

THE MOMENT SHE feels something stir inside her, she knows she doesn't want it. But then, life doesn't work that way.

The news breaks during their third month of marriage, when Sadie's belly clamps shut in some permanent way that yanks a howl from her mouth and tears Jason from his sleep. In order to sleep in the same bed together, Sadie has started wearing adult diapers to bed, unsexy disposables that leave rashy red rings along her inner thighs. To have sex means to unroll her body beyond the bounds of comfort, and it also means peeling the elastic band of the diaper from her otherwise youthful waist, so they don't do it. He's bought her the most expensive brand from Costco, the ones with soft pink florals etched into the synthetic microfibers, as if that matters, as if she cares. She's wearing fucking pull-ups. Her forehead is wrenched with sweat.

Dopey with sleep, they stumble to the bathroom, where Sadie gags and gags over the toilet but expels only loose coils of saliva and a few pathetic tears. Jason holds her hair, rubs small circles on her back.

It's gonna be okay, he says over and over again, but this man has never been sheared apart from the inside out.

He says, *I think I know what's happening, and it's a joyful thing.*

She, too, knows what it is as sure as she knows her own name and that she's in love with a man who's mostly useless. She pees on four pregnancy tests, and when two pink lines surface on every stick, Sadie throws her head back, laughs and laughs even though nothing is funny and every new second carries with it a new, intolerable hurt.

It doesn't make any sense, she tells Jason. *I'm still bleeding. We need to see a doctor.*

They drive to Kāneʻohe to see someone new, not a pediatrician but a gynecologist who treated Jason's older sister through two successful pregnancies and one unwanted one. The doctor is tall and smartly dressed, a Japanese woman in her midfifties with skin the shade of wet sand and a small, perky mouth. A stethoscope wreaths her neck like a hibiscus lei, and Sadie longs for nothing more than to be held by this woman. Reassured everything will be just fine.

After a series of tests, urine samples, blood draws, a needle that runs the width of her palm, Sadie clutches at her belly as the nameless something stirs and flops around inside her, confirming everything she already knows, has known for quite some time, and the doctor says, *Congratulations.*

Don't worry about the bleeding, she assures her. *Sometimes these things just happen. As far as I can tell, you and the baby both are in perfect health.*

Jason squeezes her hand with some semblance of reassurance, and then Sadie loses consciousness.

SOMETHING THE KĀNAKA maoli of old Hawai'i got right: remove the kāne from the bleeding wāhine waimaka lehua, for god's sake. Let the women rest.

THE ONLY 'OHANA she's ever known is Lopaka's. They are messy, loud drunks grafted permanently to their Ka'a'awa seclusion, and when they learn of her pregnancy months later, tūtū insists on throwing a party.

It's a nice gesture, but really not necessary, Sadie tells her mother, but Kāhea is insistent, mostly tired. She and Lopaka have stayed married for over a decade, a feat that's worn on her skeleton and nearly flattened her. *Lopaka wants this, he wants to celebrate you.* But Sadie understands this has nothing to do with her.

The four-to-be-five of them drive the Nissan over the Pali, the car heaving its age all over the paved highway. Jason holds her hand in the back seat and says, *Did you know before they built the Pali, if you wanted to get from windward to town side, you had to either hike through the Pali cliffs or canoe around the island?* He enjoys pinching snippets of facts from his undergrad classes, weaving them into tales to impress people.

Who the hell wanted to make that trek so badly? Lopaka asks. His hands are sailors' knots roped around the steering wheel.

It was actually for the windward farmers to bring their produce to people in the city. Sweet potato and pineapple and papaya. Poi and pigs, too.

All the while the thing expands inside her like rice cooked in a too-small pot.

They park on an open field of grass, where the house is bordered by a chain-link fence and fortified further by spikes of spare lumber Lopaka's father installed himself. Two Chihuahua mixes come charging out of the garage and barrel into Sadie's legs. They bark and howl, lap at her thighs. *Ouch*, she says, and Jason shoves them away.

You look so good! Glowing mama! Tūtū greets them in the front yard, honis them one at a time. A generous compliment, when Sadie is nothing more than a swollen alien, far too plump and engorged for someone barely through her second trimester. She knew so little about what it meant to be pregnant before all this; never did she think it could be this much of a burden. Already she's stitched an elastic band around the waistline of her jeans, and the pissing, the dizzy spells, the gripping cramps, the sexual longing. She chases orgasms like a feral creature in the wild. For now she has reconciled herself to this feral something, and tonight she smiles, says thank you to her tūtū and to all Lopaka's brothers and their children and wives, people she's known for years, who've watched her unravel into adulthood with little more than grunts of acknowledgment and the occasional fat joke.

As always, her tūtū has prepared an elaborate feast for a party several times its size. The gathering is held under the roof of the extension garage and across the run of fountain grass punctuated by thickets of dehydrated weeds. Plastic folding tables are draped in paper towels, their ripply surfaces obscured by takeout poke containers, bowls filled with pancit and pork guisantes, the crusts of lechon that always cut away at Sadie's gums. Inside, an uncle deep-fries lumpia stuffed with ground pork, water chestnuts, the snap of fresh ginger. Overripe bananas sit on a cutting board sliced into coins, browning, waiting to be rolled into dessert.

Empty Heineken bottles amass around the legs of folding tables. The night is eerily still, the chirping of geckos echoing through the garage. The dogs chase Sadie all evening, sniffing out the meat she lumbers around under the veil of belly, scratching at her legs with their untrimmed nails. The smell of fried pork, ground pork simmering on the stove, pork folded into the sleeves of lumpia wrappers, it's enough to drive her mad with nausea and also to instill in her longing—longing to be the young girl at the barbecue who's left alone to consume as much kālua pig as her heart and gut desire. She retreats from the garage to find solace in the front yard. Now Jason sits beside her in the field of grass, his cross-legged posture wrinkling his khakis. He rubs her knee, leaving splotches of grease streaked on her skin. Sadie eats from the vegetable tray, a tiny scoop of white rice and ginger for the spicy burst of flavor.

The family finds her and crowds her. They ask about her due date. She lies and says early March, though the doctor never gave them a date, not one she can remember. Strange, really, though something about the stir within her had suggested March, so this is what she told Jason, told her parents and now the extended 'ohana, and they seem pleased, a date that makes sense. They nod and eat their food, the air exhaling a curious chill. The dogs are going crazy now, yelping and hopping around, getting lickins from the uncles and from Lopaka, too. One of the cousins asks if she's having a baby boy or baby girl. She says it's impossible to know.

While the aunties clear the tables, that same cousin returns, a pretty young thing with long, slight arms and a beach tan coating her skin. She's seven, maybe eight, and she fills her fingers with Sadie's brown hair, snagging tangles on her finger. She asks Sadie if she can feed the baby a snack. Sadie shrugs and says, *Why not.*

The girl turns on her heel and sprints toward the house, the screen door slamming on its rusted track. Jason smiles at her. *I hope we have a girl*, he says and kisses her forehead in a way that makes her feel safe. Safe, with a monster growing inside her. *A girl as sweet and playful as her, as beautiful as you.*

I think it will be a boy, she lies. Lopaka's mother brings out dessert—two chocolate dobash cakes and a mango-haupia pie and a pyramid of freshly fried banana lumpia—and although sugar now makes her queasy, Sadie serves herself a serving of each.

She picks at the crumbly chocolate cake, the pie's brittle shortbread crust, and then something falls on her plate with a muted clatter. She chews the bite of crust, swallows without tasting it. The young cousin is staring at her, awaiting a response. But Sadie doesn't know how to respond to the dried pig's snout presented on her plate as an offering.

For the baby, the cousin says. Sadie stares at the dried snout, its uneven shape, two pockets of nostrils staring back at her. She prods each hole with her finger, brings the dead snout to her living one. Smells the tinge of metal, rust. Blood.

She drops her plate in the grass, toppling the cake and pie and horrible pig snout. Jason reaches for her, and a few uncles rise from their chairs. She falls to her knees and screams. Her fingers comb through the grass and the dirt, searching for the dried pig's snout. She cries, *Why is this happening?* But no one seems to understand the question. She peels through the tall emerald tufts and all the weeds, but the snout is gone. When she rises to her feet, the family is staring at her, at the dirt staining her knees and palms. The cousin, she sees now, is cowering behind her mother's monstrous calves. She holds a fistful of dried pigs' snouts in her hand, and the dogs snatch them up, one by one.

YOU WILL NOT *leave this house, you will not leave this bed. Anything you need, I'll get for you. But you need to rest. You cannot leave.*

Jason speaks to her like a doctor, which he assumes he is, now that he's taken her temperature and poured medicinal fluids into her mouth. He works at the Hawaiian diner, acting as her temporary replacement until Sadie has the baby and can return to work. He comes home with grease stains blooming on his shirt, his awful khaki shorts, and nurses her to health.

Bed rest doesn't last long. Within a week of her confinement, Sadie's water breaks all over the sheets. In twenty minutes, they make it to the hospital. An hour, and Sadie is admitted. They settle her in a shared room in the crowded maternity ward, where Jason plays *Candy*

Crush on his iPhone while Sadie doubles over in pain. Give it a minute, ten minutes, give it half an hour, give it a day, maybe. Who knows how long an agony such as this might last.

Twelve hours, and Sadie gives birth. She remembers nothing but the sweat and the blood, the room bending around her and her manic howls and all the tearing. She assumes this is how it's always done, in some flash of unkept memory, but her mother isn't there for her to ask. Her parents will stay in Pālolo, wait for the baby to come to them.

But when it's torn from her body, Sadie doesn't recognize it. *A baby*, she says, over and over again, while the nurse rips something bloody and disfigured from between her legs and races it to a table nearby. Sadie's left hand aches; she looks down and sees Jason's fingers coiled around her palm like a cobra constricting its prey, and for the first time since their union she feels embarrassed to be with him. When he lets go, her hand throbs with violet bruises.

Congratulations, the nurse says, approaching them. In her arms she slings around a bundle of ivory towels, spots of which are flecked with dark blood. *You have a healthy—*.

What was that? Sadie asks.

You're the mother of a healthy—.

Jason is grinning now, and because the nurse is still offering the bundle of towels to anyone who will accept it, Jason leaps forward, opens his arms, takes the towels. He brings them to Sadie, and her eyes swim glassy before she can see what's folded inside the bundle, and her breathing grows haggard, soft, then loud as crashing cymbals, then quiet again. Still. Her head tilts toward the bruise blooming on her hand. She sleeps for thirty-two hours while they stitch all her tears.

In her sleep, she dreams of the dried pig's snout. It's still lost somewhere in the grass of Kaʻaʻawa Valley, and Sadie is her little cousin, holding a fistful of snacks for the dogs. There is now something that's peeled itself from her body; still, her pelvis aches something awful. She claws through the grass until she feels the cool sop of dirt beneath her fingernails, claws through the dirt until her hands touch something soft, slightly porous, slightly moving. It breathes, and with every breath, Sadie's stomach contracts. She reaches between her legs and pulls her fingers away so the smears and crumbs of earth leak into her own blood. With blood and dirt and soil and earth on her fingers, Sadie gently gathers the buried thing in her arms, where she finally learns where the dried pig's snout was hidden. *This can't be real*, she says, but what does it matter when there is no one there to listen.

A baby, she says. *The mother of a healthy——*.

When she wakes up, Jason is asleep on the recliner beside her hospital bed, snoring loudly. Sadie reaches between her legs, but all she feels is the torn elastic of her own interior. No blood. The thing is gone, too. An empty plastic basin and rumpled sheets teasing her in its place.

LET THE WOMEN rest.

Sadie sleeps for days, for weeks, and this is not a dream—no more blood.

IT TAKES EIGHT weeks for Sadie's skin to heal, for her stitches to be removed by the doctor's swift hands. It takes less than five minutes from the moment they return to the apartment and shut their bedroom door for Jason to squander any progress her body has made to heal itself for the benefit of his own lonely orgasm. He peels the clothes from her body like rags and bends her facedown onto the mattress and fucks her from behind, coming quickly like a released spring. Just the way she likes it. Something awful about the clipping sear of pain fills her with a warmth she's always reserved for fucking, something good. They lie in bed for hours, touching each other's faces.

We have a—, he says, and Sadie no longer tries to understand.

We have a—.

Oh, and then there's the living thing in a bassinet. Always screaming, always frightfully alive. When Sadie goes over to examine it, a curious fog envelopes all the empty space, and she must sit down to keep from toppling over. A woman enters the apartment, holds the thing to Sadie's breast and instructs her on getting it to latch. Dip the head here, lower its lips away from the nipple's base, compress the areola; *this is as much your job as it is the living thing's.* Something sharp clamps down on her nipple, and Sadie yelps freely. At some point the woman leaves, and still the thing does not latch. Sadie leaves it to howl itself to sleep in the bassinet while she fixes herself a ham and cheese sandwich on seeded bread.

Sadie eats and sleeps and learns to tolerate the cacophony around her, but when Jason returns from work, he does so with gales of lust swarming around him, and then her job transitions to lover, wife, bad woman. She is such a nasty, bad little girl. He lays on top of her and clenches her jaw in his hand so tight she tastes blood. Falls queasy with lust and terror. *Let's make another little—*, he whispers one night, but Sadie hears only the enduring cries tenting their bedroom.

The blood, oh, how it once lived as a companion in her body! Now just a smear of sludge she holds inside her when Jason fucks her too hard. No other part of her bleeds, at least not in ways that're visible to others. Would it be better, she wonders, in between the living thing's lamentations and Jason's new insatiability, if she simply continued to bleed in the same interminable fashion? Would she be more like herself, the person she always intended to be?

It's a loss, then. She runs her fingers along the cotton lining of her underwear and feels only fabric and thinks, *Yes, a loss.* A loss she is far too young to understand, won't understand for years and years.

That's how long it feels as though she's slept. The next time she wakes up, she does so to her fists curled around the sheets, a stiff cotton fabric wilted dank with sweat. In the dark corner of the room, the bassinet glows as though someone's kindled it to life. She hesitates to sit up entirely, and when she finally does, when she swings her legs over the edge of the mattress, her steps come slackened, almost timid. The bassinet is five hundred miles away and just across the room. When she peers her head over the frame, the living thing is gone, and only a muted breath leaves her chest. She reaches into the bassinet, clutches a miniature wild hog, a pua'a she knows, its coat soaked in blood that stains her dress, her arms, and then her neck as she hugs it close to her chest, ignoring the bristle of its hair on her bare skin, its animalistic shrieks, listening only to the orchestra of heartbeats as the creature stills in her arms.

She turns to see Jason fixed in the doorway, color seeping from his unfamiliar face.

She is crying, and she can't stop smiling.

We have a—.

Story of Men

The day we put the dryer out on the street was the day the Menehune showed its face. Leimomi had purchased it used at a neighborhood tūtū's estate sale, but it was George who decreed the dryer nothing more than a piece of junk, its lint catcher dewy with mold, its knobs axles of rust. Most importantly, the drum was far too small to accommodate the linens of two parents and six keiki. No ordinary dryer would do; a kānaka 'ohana demanded a kānaka dryer.

But Leimomi resented the waste of money. She was old-school Hawaiian, which meant anything with a fingerprint on the 'āina was still salvageable. Including this hunk-of-junk appliance. She would prove it to George, ever the skeptic; restore the thing to its vintage gleam.

She foraged through the untilled yard and the cluttered carport, and when she went to retrieve the dryer from the sidewalk she saw the door had been opened and, inside, a baby.

No, not a baby. Something else.

Lying fetal in the corner of the drum, the thing stirred. Its dark eyes narrow as papaya seeds, its lips full and smeared in blood. No, not blood—she examined it closer and saw the burnished currant was simply its native shade. The rest of it, naked and richly tanned. The realization lashed at her that this thing with its smooth, mature face bore the body of a newborn, and how could something so monstrous also appeal to her as beautiful?

She reached into the dryer. The thing did not flinch when she folded her fingers around its bare belly. Didn't parry her arms away or make to cry. She brought it to the light and only then did it object, its adult face cinching into a tight grimace, so she hurried to the carport, where she could catch some shade. She felt the thing repose in her arms.

Girl One and Two whapped at the screen door, their rubber slippers *slap-slapping* the hot asphalt under their feet.

Leimomi hushed them.

We need to be thoughtful. We need to let it sleep.

But the girls pulled and tugged at her forearms, pressing, crying, so much so they attracted the attention of their brothers, Boys One and Three and Four, and their pawing fingernails left deep scrawls spoked into Leimomi's skin and how she cried out, for they were hurting her! Only upon sensing Leimomi's pain did the thing let out a cry that reached into her own throat and recovered a wool of her singular, curious suffering.

The keiki muffled their ears with their hands.

It was a cry that tore caws from the feral roosters' jowls, a cry that reached even Boy Two, the troubled child, below the Nimitz bridge, where he smoked pakalolo and set several strange fires with his buddies. Cars shuttled above him, tires screaming and engines sputtering, and still he could hear that cry in a way that might've tugged him home, had he not been strung out and too proud like his pops. No matter, because eventually the thing stopped crying, and Girl Two sprinted away from their huddle just as Boy Four pawed at Leimomi's curled arms, asked with his soft eyes if he could hold the baby, and she had to correct him then—*this is not a baby*—and he questioned—*then what is it?*—and before she could answer, Girl Two returned with a quilted pillowcase, emerald monstera leaves embossed in the stitching, and she explained—*for the baby*—and then Leimomi sighed, seized by a rote sadness and desperate longing for George to help her as she repeated—*this is not a baby*—and Girl Two asked—*then what is it?*—and Leimomi replied—*it's a Menehune.*

EVERYTHING SHE KNEW about Menehune she had gleaned from her tūtū, dead now. Would you believe there is no widely accepted understanding of these magical beings? Some wield the legend as a cautionary tale for their kolohe keiki—*You act up li'dat and the Menehune go'n turn you to stone.* Others print cartoonish caricatures of Menehune malo-garbed and lei'd as company mascots; treat them like cuddly elves bearing beach tans and good cheer. The Menehune of her tūtū, however, were of a different class entirely. These were Hawai'i's master builders, the skilled engineers who crafted entire loko i'a, stone heiau overnight and out of nothing. Laborers of the 'āina. Only in oral legend were they said to be tiny, though now with Men in the house, Leimomi had come to realize such narratives might in fact be built on something solid.

Men was not the name we assigned her but the name she gave herself. Men lived on fingers of poi and apple bananas and required total darkness to sleep. She padded through the house barefoot and naked while none of us bothered to drape her in our contemporary modesty. We left her alone. She took supreme care in examining every messy room, every trench of space in our too-tiny hale before settling back in the dryer, now pitched under the carport between the washer and a rusted sink we never used. Slept there the first night and left the door open, and the next morning, when Leimomi went to inspect the work required to restore the appliance, she found the dryer revived in its second life! Haloed in light and standing on brand-new spokes. She peered inside the drum. There was Men, supine, asleep.

More was restored, after that. We went off to school and faked at paying attention to our kumu, and when we came home our busted shower door was refastened to its hinges. In the kitchen, the drawer that was always acting up had been washed clean of the syrupy gunk ladling its runners, now opening and closing without even a groan or sigh. Outside, the unwoven clothesline spun back into itself, slung across the yard stable and taut. Even the finicky light suspended in the hall closet now blinked anew. We didn't understand it. We toed around Men and knew from the recognition punching down our spines she was working overtime on the hale as the rest of the house slept.

Of our entire 'ohana, George was Men's favorite.

But of course, Leimomi needed her more. She couldn't comprehend Men's affection toward George—that quiet, curmudgeonly soul who hadn't even found her!—and why Lei's own attempts at tenderness were met only with Men's blank stares. Lei, she did the best she could. Pampered the dryer's empty drum with quilts and sheets and pillows puffed by her own fists and even left daily a hand of apple bananas plucked from our tree for Men to snack on as she pleased. Men pleased not. Early morning, and Leimomi found the linens tossed haplessly on the asphalt of the carport, laked in motor oil. Men, elsewhere. She searched and searched the yard, calling her name. When she found Men indoors, ensconced in the top drawer of George's dresser, cradled in the elastic band of his boxer briefs, snoring softly, she pressed her fingers to Men's temples and pretended her own heart wasn't quaking in her chest.

Because of the rarity of Men's existence, George contemplated calling reporters. Because she exercised more than half her brain, Leimomi insisted on his silence. Men must be protected.

You're welcome to stay as long as you like, but Men grew and grew. Soon she could no longer fit inside the dryer's barrel, and George took to building her a private oasis where our outhouse once sat. For the master builder, he built her walls of thatched bamboo, a ceiling of palm fronds stitched together by twine. He carved a little cutout for a window, salvaged a mattress from the street and positioned it so that neither Men's head nor Men's feet addressed the window or the door. He foraged Boy Two's bedroom—who knew whether or when the son might make his return?—from which he pilfered downy pillows, a ceramic bowl once filled with pakalolo leaves, a framed photograph of Lē'ahi rising its vertiginous emerald heads into the sky. Poor Leimomi. How many years of meticulous care she'd extended into his hovel, the shrine of Boy Two that still nursed her grief, where she prayed he might one day soon return! How the ache must've pushed down her throat like a brick.

Leimomi needed to care for someone. Her keiki were all either too needy or too independent, while George, in his old age, was evolving into another person entirely.

Loose-limbed and weary, George snarled easy at the kids and even more easily at his wife, his patience a string tuned tight to snapping. Yes, age had weathered his body and his mind, but it had also weathered his composure, leaving him a fiction of the man who'd once wooed her. And while he never lifted a hand to his 'ohana, those scowling bursts of dissention pushed his presence in the house toward intolerable. With Men, Leimomi was given a second chance, a chance to live her life for someone else and to finally do it right.

You're welcome to stay for a while, but tell me, where did you come from?

FOR WEEKS, MEN didn't speak. This is how we entered a soft season of watching Men eat fistfuls of dirt from the backyard, where George had made her home.

In the beginning, Leimomi did her best to put an end to things. Panic knuckled down her spine at that first sighting, and so Lei leapt into solutions mode, delivering Men bowls of mango wedges, papaya peeled and seeded for quick consumption. Two-finger poi, Men's preferred consistency. She brought Men liters of water with glacial ice cubes and a carton of Passion Orange Guava she stored in a disposable foam cooler, the only one we could afford. Everything left melted, dejected and untouched, under the slatted ceiling of palm fronds. Lei ventured outside two, three times a day, peering through the bamboo thatching. Clots of dirt caught around Men's mouth, the mud bleeding into her own brown tan.

Most of us had lost interest in Men at that point. Only Girl Two persisted, fascination boiling in both thumbs. Because she also happened to be George's favorite, Girl Two was in a relatively privileged position to befriend Men. Men, for all her dirt and twig consumption, had also persisted with her master building. Every morning, we woke to the relentless pitch of the roosters and some new home fixture upended and repaired. The curling linoleum in the living room now ironed flat; the garbage disposal unjammed; cracked grout unfractured; gate latch repaired. All the while she was consuming mud, heaps and heaps pulled from the earth. Men built solutions into the floorboards of our home. Girl Two watched.

Leimomi worried. She didn't know how to reach the girl—and could she even call her a girl? Him, them, it? Or was Leimomi now contending with someone, something, possibly unhuman? And still, how many times her tūtū had to remind her—Menehune were the original Hawaiian people! People. So why did Men insist on eating bowls of dirt?

George cared. Didn't know any better than his wife, but of course he assumed he did. Great Big Man with a capital *M*. Men was softening all his corners. One day, after a particularly heated outburst had jumped from his wife's throat, George paid a visit to Men's new home. Standing outside the bamboo walls, he admired his creation. Inside, Men slept. George didn't dare enter without permission, but something must've rustled under his feet, then, perhaps a notch of twigs, for well before he could even entertain the idea of knocking, the door opened. He passed through. Men sat cross-legged on a square of Leimomi's hand-stitched quilt, regarding him.

Girl Two huddled behind the mango tree, eavesdropping.

You want to know why I'm here, while your wife wants to know how long I intend to stay. These were the first words proffered by Men; her tone simmered, her cadence compressed into a tight fist.

You're welcome to stay—

But she cut him off. *The truth is, I'm not welcomed to stay anywhere. Have you asked yourself the simple questions your wife is asking? Where did I come from? Why your house, your old, abandoned dryer? Have you wondered after the rest of us?*

The rest of you? Really he wondered about not much but what he stared at were her breasts, hung slackened and uncaged like the feral chickens rooting around their yard. No shoot of lust pushed through him. Call it curiosity, or admiration. Like Leimomi, he aimed to protect her.

The Menehune generations. We have been here, we belong here. For centuries before the arrival of man, Menehune made a community on the foothills of Waimea Valley. You locals think we're only little people, dwarfs, elves from the pictures. You've made us into a joke. Our story is one you will never know, because the rest of us, the ones who stayed, we're forbidden from sharing.

Girl Two leaned in closer, pushing the boundaries of the mango trunk.

You can tell me, said George. *Is it true you turn men to stone? I want to know everything about you. You can tell me. I'm a trustworthy person.*

You may think that, but what about me? You men, always thinking of yourselves and never how you might flip a question around. The truth is, I am not someone worthy of your trust. Will you trust me anyway? Most likely. I could tell you about my father, a king among Menehune and the first man to gut a wild boar with a spear built by his own hands. I could tell you about my mother, a Hawaiian woman. I could tell you the dozens of ways the Menehune council made it impossible for such crossbreeding to persist and what exactly happened to my mother, what grisly fate she bore. I could shock you with language of the macabre—do you wince at the words slit slice strangle carve claw cut butcher bury rape ravage bleed? *Should I go on?*

Shards of human voice splintered down the side of the house then, and George stirred. Elsewhere, Girl Two stumbled. Hooked her leg around a jutting root of the mango tree then fell flat on her face.

Should I go on?

So ended the soft season, the dirt eating, the not speaking.

YOU'RE WELCOME TO stay, but please, do not hurt us.

AND ALTHOUGH MEN wouldn't dare hurt us, things shifted around the house all the same. What she'd repaired during the weeks of her stay, Men reversed overnight. The shower door, unhinged; the clothesline unwoven and dragged to the gravel like unspun hair. Our lightbulbs burst at odd and irreverent times. What pooled grief into Leimomi's heart, though, was the dryer: newly eclipsed in a familiar rust, the dryer stopped working. The lint catcher showing seasons of dust.

She even dismantled the hale George had built for her.

It was Girl Two who found her for the last time. We watched her watching Men's comings and goings from her square of window in the bedroom Girls One and Two shared with Boy Four. She pinched between her tiny fingers the barrels of the used binoculars, also foraged from tūtū's estate sale, and peeled the landscape for any motion of Men. Men's short, angular limbs. There. Rooted to the soil like a captain surveying her wreckage, Men sat among stacks of sifted bamboo, bundles of twine, fractured petioles of palm fronds. Folds of skin pushed together near her middle like the pleats of an accordion. She lifted her face to the sun. She didn't move. Girl Two, neither. She watched Men breathe air into her lungs (did she have lungs?) and stir something solid in her heart (did she have a heart?), and some invisible pressure pressed into Girl Two's side and it told her the truth: *Time's up.*

So still Men sat, Girl Two could've sworn Men found a way to turn herself to stone.

MEN LEFT. WE blamed ourselves; we blamed each other.

George's fault for forcing Men into speech, and Leimomi's fault for not saying enough. Girl One's fault for showing no interest. Boy Two's fault for always being elsewhere, leaving us lonely and in a lurch. Boy Four's fault, and Girl Two's. The truth is, we were all at fault, for either loving too much or not loving quite enough.

Would you believe it if we told you Girl Two never recovered? So many years later, and still none of us can say with confidence what made her most susceptible to Men, or what Men wanted from her. Regardless, she wanted too much. And Girl Two, too, how she drowned in an awful longing! What use would she make of those binoculars now? For so long, Men was hers to watch and wait for. Now Men is gone, and Girl Two colonizes that freighted patch of land with her knees hugged to her chest, her shirt stripped off in Men's likeness, and what would the neighbors say? We watched Girl Two. She sat there for what felt like hours, days, feeling around for her immense loss then feeling nothing, not moving, immobile, ground down, rooted, stone.

But Men, she hasn't stopped moving.

Can you see her now, traveling on foot to another 'ohana in another house? Can you see her gentle footfalls? The way she holds her breasts with callous resolve? Do you see her curl inside cupboards, stairwells, wall crawls, rapacious for cover, privacy, space? The 'ohana she visits change with the seasons; Men never does. Do you see how it is now?

Do you look her straight in the eyes? Work tirelessly to contain her?

Are you afraid yet?

Have you stilled to stone?

Temporary Dwellers

With this new girl, I figure the best way to keep at things is to pretend she is related to me. This is not some implausible scenario. We are Hawaiian Japanese haole, the both of us, with wiry black hair and skin the shade of overturned coral. She could be a distant third cousin, or the daughter my mother abandoned at birth.

She could be all these things, and still that does not stop me from waking in the middle of the night with my hands in my underwear, groping around like a physician giving a pelvic exam. There are so many things I don't know about my body, how certain soft spots make me shudder while others flush me with fear. Sometimes I tug my hands out from the sheets and cup them against the wall, listening to the girl's muffled sounds as she pads across the carpet, opens and closes drawers, turns on the air conditioner, locks her door with a soft click.

In the mornings, it's hard to say whether I've done something shameful or stayed exactly the same.

This girl is my mother's latest charity case, a former Kauaʻi resident fleeing the bombs, and she is not very polite. She says *fuck* a lot and leaves half-eaten bowls of cereal curdling in the sink. She ignores the dog when it claws at her knees, ignores my mother's saccharine small talk, stands in the shower for half an hour, an hour, letting scalding hot water wash over her skin and watching her long strands of hair spiral down the drain. She leaves the bathroom and says, *There's no more hot water.* She asks my mother to buy an expensive brand of cereal you can find only at Whole Foods. She says *Thank you*, while staring sullenly at her feet.

Of course, she isn't all bad. She loans me a silk blouse that makes my breasts look buoyant and inviting, and she doesn't ask me why I don't have a boyfriend when everyone else at the academy is paired off. On the nights when I listen to her through the bedroom wall, closing the jalousies and breathing heavily, I am stockpiling evidence of her temporary dwelling in this house.

A few weeks into her tenancy, and I'm sitting on the kitchen counter scooping papaya meat with my fingers and asking my mother why, if the Kauaʻi bombing will soon end, do we keep accepting the island's former residents into our home?

She doesn't answer me right away. She wipes down the countertop with bleach and a new sponge and then she asks, "Who says the bombing will ever end?" Sometimes my mother depresses me. She thinks she's being compelling and cryptic, when really she is just as confused as the rest of us.

WHEN SCHOOL STARTS up again, the girl comes with me. We are in the same homeroom, the same AP World History class, and at the end of the day we catch the city bus to Kalihi and sit next to each other, not speaking. I glance at her only when I'm convinced she's committed her attention elsewhere. She wears a vacant expression and sharp cheekbones that arch like inverted parentheses. Her skin is pale for a Hawaiian, her eyes are dark and expressionless. Like someone's sopped the life out of her.

In September, I invite her to a party. She's been with us for a few months now, and I am walloped by a sense of duty to make her feel welcome, however belatedly. We collide near the bathroom, and with my toothbrush rooting around in my mouth I tell her my sort-of-friend Dennis is having a party in Kahala and I ask if she'd like to come with me. She's wearing a flimsy maroon T-shirt and gray underwear, her eyes cloudy with sleep. She shrugs and says "Sure," and then she pivots around me to the bathroom and I hear the door lock quickly.

My mother commends my hospitality in the kitchen. She feeds me nonfat yogurt sprinkled with cinnamon and a cold glass of Passion Orange Guava. She turns the television down low until it's barely audible, and together we coalesce into the flashing imagery of the morning news report. Grim news, only, always. When the Kauaʻi bombings started not so long ago, most everyone thought it was some elaborate practical joke, a big-bellied laugh for the USA at kānaka expense. It seemed outrageous to imagine the Garden Island under attack—an occupied land being reoccupied for military training. The kūpuna lounged in their koa rocking chairs and laughed. Now no one is laughing.

On the news now rolls home video of this morning's bombing, the fourth incident this week. The screen goes black, silent, and then a quick clap of color detonates without warning, and someone says something that's censored, probably *oh fuck* or *shit's fucked up*. The station loops the same eight-second clip over and over again, and then my mother turns off the television.

The girl is standing behind us in a tight black ensemble and rubber slippers. Thick mascara clumps her long lashes. The backpack strap looped over her shoulder is worn and fraying. She stares at us for a moment before leaving for the bus without me.

THE NEWS ANCHORS, the pundits, the incensed:

"The U.S. Army and U.S. Navy have officially been granted access to the southern boundary of Kauaʻi to be utilized as a bombing range and military training site. All residents within the boundary's perimeter have been notified of their required immediate evacuation. Hawai'i representatives are currently negotiating with U.S. leaders to arrange housing for the displaced, though no formal agreement has been reached . . ."

"Although the strikes originated from the U.S. military's desperate need for an undisturbed training site, they've certainly taken on the skin of a heinous crime committed against the Hawaiian people. At this time, there are only four designated safe zones on Kaua'i that aren't vulnerable to the strikes. We're calling on the U.S. government to intervene before our island crumbles to dust . . ."

"The strikes are imperative to the advancement of the U.S. military and the long-term security of the American people. We are deeply saddened by the situation on Kaua'i, but find it a necessary sacrifice for the larger goal of training our armed forces to defend the American people against outside invasions, by any means necessary . . ."

"You snakes went slither on the memory of our kūpuna and then you going throw up your hands and say you never went do nothing wrong? Shame on you. We give all our aloha to you guys and you still gon' screw us over like snakes . . ."

"Should the U.S. military continue to pursue its current course of action, we will be forced to retaliate by any means necessary. Nothing short of a complete withdrawal from the island will assuage Kānaka Maoli of Hawai'i . . ."

And it goes on and on and on.

THE PARTY IS held in a gated Kahala estate where German-engineered cars dimple the streets and an elaborate koi pond greets us at the entrance. Outside, a couple I don't recognize have their hands in each other's back pockets and are kissing. The girl is standing beside me, our elbows touching. Misty sheets of cool rain blow over us, the breeze abrading our good hair. I watch the koi swimming in frantic circles, dodging the displays of artificial coral invading their underwater home. The massive koa door to the house opens, slams shut, opens again.

"Dennis has a very wealthy stepmother," I explain to the girl, but she's on her phone, not looking at me. We step over the mound of sandals, sneakers, slippers collected on the rubber mat fronting the entryway and venture forward.

Inside, the house thrums with a thrilling sort of youthful hysteria that zaps my breath just standing on the hardwood floors. Kids I recognize from the academy swarm the kitchen and living room, necks of cheap beer bottles dangling from their fingers, sweat lacing their foreheads. The whole house is saturated by thick clouds of pakalolo smoke, and a salty breeze blows in from the waters off Portlock. I see Dennis standing over a folding table propped open in the hallway, rubbing his chin, staring at the playing cards in his hand. When he sees us, he grins and waves to me and the girl. He has coarse black hair and speaks with a heavy pidgin accent. He asks if he can get us some beers, and we await his return with our arms crossed.

The girl has her fingers glued to her phone like it's an extension of her own physical body, and for this I am grateful. It's so much easier to stare at her when she pays me no regard. Her wide eyes are streaked heavy with mint green eye shadow; her lips are painted plum. The silver and diamond studs lining her left ear's thin cartilage flicker under the living room's harsh overheads. I'm staring, and the sound system pulses and *thud-thuds* overhead, and Dennis slips a beer in my hand, and the girl lifts her head and locks me in her gaze and says, "Your mother's a little crazy, huh?"

I take a big sip from the Heineken bottle and feel the liquid slurp and sizzle down my throat. Someone bumps against my shoulder. In the hallway behind us, some girl is screeching something about the keg, the keg! I see a slow smile spread across the girl's face. She isn't wrong. I say, "Yes, I guess."

"I don't mean she isn't nice. But she taped photos of the Nāpali Coast on my window when we were at school yesterday. She said when I look out the window, she wants me to see my homeland as it was before the bombs. That's a little kooky. I mean, they're not even bombing the North Shore yet."

I laugh; I can't help it. The beer feels so good, and I rarely drink in front of beautiful people, and Dennis keeps coming over to flirt with the girl but she's only talking to me. He's not even in her line of sight.

Miffed, Dennis shuffles away as I lean into the doorframe and recount a story I didn't know I still held room for in my mind, a tale of elementary school me and single-mother Gina visiting the Nāpali Coast for the first time. Though neither of us could boast a cultivated athleticism, my mother for months had fixated on hiking the Kalalau Trail, a voyage of several days through narrow valleys and sharp, steep switchbacks that daunt even the most experienced hikers. I don't remember how old I was, but I do remember the awkward way I'd jut my feet out sideways when I'd walk, waddling as if to complement my chunky arms and soft pouch of stomach. A mere mile into the hike, and I was already huffing, my lungs draining air into the ether like the guts of a squeezed lime. There was a young haole couple trailing us, and at some point the guy snickered, and my mother just lunged, tearing the unfashionable fanny pack from her hips and walloping him in the head with the loaded pouch. She demanded he apologize to me, and then I gagged a few times before vomiting all over his shoes, the whole thing a miasma of shame and regret.

I don't know what this story is meant to say about my mother. I finish my beer at the end of my tale and feel something snarl deep in my gut as the girl presses me against the wall, brings her beer bottle to my cheek, watches drops of condensation roll down my face, kisses me hard where the water streaks my skin. I hold my breath. All my past notions of her unfurl somewhere deep in my cunt, and my legs split open, and she slips right through.

WEEKS LATER, AND they are still bombing, and it is still raining, the stillness of our home punctuated by the *plop plop* of raindrops torrenting the tin shingles overhead. My mother is in her bedroom, or padding around the kitchen, or running errands around town, and the girl is curled up beside me, snoring loudly, dark hair draped over her face like a mask. I don't dare touch her. I stare at her smooth forehead and the rings under her eyes and see my own reflection saddled beside me. I dip my nose into the milky-soft fabric of her nightgown and wonder how long I might keep her.

Together, we are quiet and still. She slips her hand in my underwear, and I breathe heavily into her face. When she rises, she does so in wide, looping motions. To evade my mother, she tiptoes around the house and keeps an extra set of clothes buried under my academy uniform. We talk about my mother, or we don't say anything at all.

In the kitchen, we eat poached eggs and toast with lilikoi jelly and we watch reporters relay the most recent casualties of the bombings, now traveling north: a family of four in the Wailua Homesteads, an elderly couple that refused to evacuate their Anahola home. Toppled horse corpses litter the trail to a Kōloa stable, their bodies distended, swollen with trapped blood. Egg yolk trickles down the girl's lip, and I have to sit on my hands to keep from swiping at it with my fingers.

The news anchor: "The entire island is now under a mandatory evacuation, save for the communities of Hanalei and Princeville. We expect the president will make a statement this afternoon on what we all hope will be an end to such widespread devastation . . ."

The girl: "It's fucking hopeless."

My mother: turns off the television.

AT THE ACADEMY, girls stick fingers down their throats and vomit in the lockers of their enemies. They link arms and whisper either benign secrets or incendiary fantasies in each other's ears. They walk with a guilty spring in their step, conscious they are on the saved island, that they were spared for no justifiable reason. They watch me and the girl walking through the halls, not touching.

It's a strange thing, to be in love during a national crisis.

I would like to talk to the girl in class, in the halls, in the kitchen, in bed, but there isn't a lot to say, just as there is so much skin to explore. We skip homeroom and pass the time in the girls' bathroom, where I hold her face in my hands, feel my own cheeks flush bright red. In the dimly lit stall, she straddles my lap over the toilet seat and covers my mouth with her palm. Sometimes a door creaks open, and a toilet flushes, and girls giggle and coo just outside our stall, but this doesn't stop her from unbuckling my belt and grinding against my pelvis until I'm shuddering gasps through the slits in her fingers.

One afternoon, the vice principal summons me to his office to say I've missed too many classes. It's the same day the newspaper announces the birth of a Native Hawaiian coalition to reclaim Kaua'i. He sits high on his perch behind a massive koa desk, and above his balding head is a framed portrait of Kaumuali'i, the last ruling king of Kaua'i, the ali'i after whom the academy is named. In the painting, Kaumuali'i is depicted in the august mahiole and a resplendent red feather ahu ula and he is frowning. The vice principal is also frowning. He places his thick-rimmed glasses on the desk and clicks and unclicks a ballpoint pen. He says, "These unexcused absences are unacceptable," and "You're an excellent student but you're making poor choices," and "I'd hate to see you influenced negatively by your peers," and he says all these things while Kaumuali'i's ghost tugs loose from the portrait and hovers overhead. I want to ask the vice principal how he manages to separate the daily operations of the academy from what's happening on Kaua'i, *to* Kaua'i, how he can place one foot in front of the other while his school's namesake buckles under blow after blow, each bomb a shank to the gut. I want to ask him if he will be joining the coalition, if he's taking the girl with him.

I ask him instead to excuse my absences. I promise him cooperation, perfect attendance, a positive attitude; I solemnly swear to be the perfect student.

He writes me up anyway. I show the girl the detention slip in my bedroom, and she drops to the carpet on her knees, peeling my underwear from my hips. Her fingernails are painted red; the paint is chipping. I moan and listen for my mother.

LATER, THE GIRL and my mother are standing in the kitchen, arguing. I slink through the hallway and hide behind the splintering china hutch. The television is still on but the sound is off. I watch the talking heads on TV open and close their mouths so wide I hear their jaws clicking in the back of my skull.

"You think I'm broken or bad, but I'm *fine*." The girl is leaning against the refrigerator, arms folded across her chest. I watch my mother shake her head, wield a butter knife in the air like a police baton.

"You're traumatized," she says. "I can see it on your face."

I chew on the pillowy insides of my cheeks until I taste rust-sour blood. I listen to their verbal sparring, tally their points in my head. I don't even need to hear the words to know they are arguing about the Kaua'i coalition. The girl would like to join. My mother would like the girl to see a therapist. Neither is thrilled with the other, and their argument sends sparks of pain shooting off from the back of my skull.

"You don't get a say in how I choose to fight back." The girl stares my mother down with the same rigid intensity with which she'd pinned me to the wall in Kahala, but unlike her pliant daughter, my mother doesn't flinch.

"You're staying away from the coalition, and you're going to this appointment. You need to talk to someone about your family, and clearly you won't talk to me or my daughter, who has been nothing but welcoming to you since the day you got here. You're going, or you can find yourself a new place to stay."

I turn away.

I listen to the girl's heavy footfalls up the carpeted stairs, down the hall. The door slams, and my mother whimpers, dropping the knife in the sink with a sharp clang.

Upstairs, the girl lies facedown on the sheets, wearing nothing but baggy cotton underwear and my old Rainbow Warriors Volleyball shirt, the white one with a hole under the breast. I close the door behind me gently, lock it. She rises to her knees and tilts her head a little to the side. I climb onto the churning mattress. She rubs slow circles on my thigh with her thumb. I hold a fistful of her curls in my hand, and I marvel over how I got so lucky, how everything has gone so terribly wrong.

"Are you really joining the coalition? Are you leaving?" I want to saw my own lips off for sounding so desperate.

"Your mother seems to think so," she says.

"I can talk to her later," I offer. "Calm her down a little."

But the girl is shaking her head back and forth, eyes closed. I know so little of this girl who looks like me, whose entire past life has been ushered forward as a sacrifice for an American cause we don't understand. And anyway, I care so little for America; I only want her hands on my chest.

I stare at her for a long time, neither of us touching the other. She brings a clump of my dehydrated curls to her mouth, sucks on the stiff tips. I ask her to tell me about her family on Kaua'i. But the girl has other ideas, one of which is to yank me down on the sheets by my hair, our troubles splayed out like our own bodies on this warm bed.

TO MY KNOWLEDGE, the bombing does not end. People simply lose interest in talking about it.

Winter rolls through the islands in quick bursts of torrential rain, manic thunderstorms, then stillness. The girl and I hide under the banyan trees in Waikīkī until the sun sets, then we amble to the beach in our bathing suits and rubber slippers. We sit on the coral jetty and point at the shipping containers churning leisurely southward. Point at haole tourists sunburnt frightfully, and at a hāpai white woman chained by a closed-flower lei and stroking her belly. We dip our heads under the salt water, letting it cleanse us of our sins. At all hours of the night, tourists wander the pebbled shoreline, so we save the fucking for her bedroom, once my mother falls asleep.

Her body beside me is a phantasmal thing, and I feel her slinking away as easy as the current tugging loose from the shore.

A few blocks from the banyan trees, we chase each other around a grassy field, our slippers getting caught in the soil's mottled depressions. We collapse when our legs and lungs give way, the somber shadow of Lē'ahi looming over us, wrapping us in shadows. I stare at the girl. A nest of golden weeds collects just above her head; she looks as though she's been crowned. I think of all the words that have been used to describe the Kaua'i coalition, its members still intent on taking back their land: *empowered, irrational, organized, mysterious, embittered, vindictive, dangerous.* Then I think of all the words I would use to describe this girl beside me, and the words don't change.

Quietly I assemble the weeds like an art piece, burying them in the loose clusters of her curls. She glances up, laughs. I want to bottle her laugh and send it off to sea, or keep it hidden in one of my dresser drawers, an archive of her time here.

She holds my hand and stares at the blue sky, the clouds passing overhead. "I'm leaving," she says. She won't look at me, but I can't stop staring at her, combing her eyes and lips and skin for some sincerity grafted to these two simple words. For a while we say nothing, and she appears to feel nothing, and there are myna birds screeching in the shower trees above us, and a car alarm ripping through the open field.

I take a breath, and the only word that comes to me is *fuck*. I say it aloud.

The girl laughs and says, "Fuck, indeed." Then she rolls on top of me, wipes the sweat from my forehead.

"When do you leave?" I ask.

A slow smile spreads across her face. "Let's just do what we do best and not talk about it."

DAYS, WEEKS PASS, and we don't talk about it. We tread water in the sticky basin of Kailua Beach and eat Spam musubi from a truck stop and drink copious amounts of Coca-Cola and have lots of sex on the soft queen bed the girl will soon vacate. We watch the news at full volume once my mother leaves for work. We take nude photos with an old Polaroid I excavated from the basement then rip the prints in half and laugh.

She buys a duffel bag. It's droopily stitched from a beige fabric and has an excessive number of pockets, inside which she shoves her underwear and hair ties and tampons and ballpoint pens and bikini bottoms and passport and coin purse, a chaotic collection of her little life here. I sit cross-legged at the edge of the bed, watching her pack.

"You're not packing right," I say. "There's no system, you're just shoving things in empty pockets."

She balls a T-shirt in front of her chest, doesn't even look up. "So?"

"So, what if you have to piss really badly and you're bleeding but you can't find your fucking tampons? What are you going to do then?"

She pauses, as if seriously contemplating this outrageous scenario. "I'll use toilet paper, I guess. No big deal."

"That's disgusting."

"It's more sanitary than walking around with menstrual blood dripping down my legs," she says.

I feel the tips of my ears flush red hot. "You're disgusting. Why can't you just pack like a normal person?"

And with my hands trembling, and stomach rumbling low, and ears red-hot, I am more assured than ever before that what I want to say is something different entirely, something nurturing and vulnerable that sounds more like a plea than a shallow criticism. What I want to say is something I've rehearsed since I imagined her to be related to me just to restrain my own desires, since she ran the cool Heineken bottle over my face and slipped her fingers inside me. I'm rubbing my thighs with the soft pads of my hands. I'm staring at her like I might be able to hold her in place, like silence will somehow make our coupling permanent.

"If you're trying to tell me to stay, or that you love me or something, you're doing a shit job," she says. She tugs on a zipper to reveal another pocket, and in goes a handful of quarters, a cracked compact mirror.

SHE GOES MISSING the day a riot breaks out at the Hawaiʻi State Capitol. Those who fled Kauaʻi can't afford a plane ticket to D.C., so they settle for a civic battle, marching across the statehouse's poorly watered grounds, chanting, *Ua Mau ke Ea o ka ʻĀina i ka Pono*, until someone in a black hoodie plants what's reported to be a dirty bomb in the central atrium and the bomb squad and SWAT teams rush the scene and the whole building evacuates. The bomb never goes off. No one dies. It's almost funny, how ineffectual it all is.

When I finally notice she's gone, I'm eating a turkey wrap over the sink, finishing a problem set for math class. I'm thinking about the properties of matrix multiplication, while in the living room the news screens B-roll of coalition members fleeing the capitol, and when I race upstairs to tell the girl about the bomb, she isn't there. I flip over the comforter, open the closet door, look in the bathroom, peer behind the nightstand—nothing. I sit on the edge of the bed and hold my face in my hands.

I think about how what remains of Kauaʻi is exactly that: remains. Scattered debris, swollen carcasses, a smoky residue settled over what had once been the fiercest of the islands, the landmass with resistance settled in its soil. I consider my mother's bony hands on my shoulders, holding me in place as I stood perilously close to the Nāpali cliff. I marvel over how I am always finding a precipice, always looking for the nearest ledge to try my luck. I think about the girl's hands inside me, and the soft sounds she made in this bedroom next to mine.

The door creaks slightly, and the girl walks in holding the duffel bag to her chest. A black hoodie dangles from the crook in her elbow. "Now I really gotta go," she says softly. I see her, and something cracks in the base of my throat, and she rushes forward and holds me for a long time. I don't know who I will be once this girl slips out from under me, though I suspect it won't be much longer before I find out.

Madwomen

My son, Toby, demands many stories, but it's the story of the Madwoman he likes best. Because he is part Hawaiian and often forgets, I have made her the Madwoman in the Sea—some foolish attempt to right him with his ʻāina.

I tuck my son into the swaddle of his trundle bed, cup the tender tissue of his cheek, which glows the shade of spoiled milk.

Legend claims Her as its own manic invention—brilliant, beautiful, disillusioned, a little lonely. They say She is a beguiling young thing with tendrils of seaweed for hair and two rows of cuspate teeth like upturned blades wedged in perpetually bleeding gums. Her closest companion is the inimitable tiger shark, *Galeocerdo cuvier*; Her lover is the spindly wana concealed in the dark coral landscape. She emerges often and at random; a harbinger of death and storms, of illicit activity, of doom. A product of young boys who refuse to brush their teeth before bedtime, boys who defy their mothers or speak ill of their absent fathers.

He demands I slow down and use smaller words. But this is my tale to tell, and I will tell it as I please.

The Madwoman in the Sea bears twelve eyes stippled over a tawny face. She is always watching; when one eye closes, eleven eyes peel open to take notes. For centuries, surfers and divers have composed wild narratives of taming the Madwoman with a soft kiss on her forked tail, which is dressed in millions of diamond scales, each one a dagger poised to slay. Legend claims if you survive this kiss of death, you have not only tamed the Madwoman, but you have also achieved immortality.

(I don't know where I come up with these lies.)

Creeping along the turquoise undertow, She is all tempest and commotion, an effulgent vapor of light that lures not only miniature fish but also unsuspecting men and children—the very surfers and divers who proclaim with jolly-happy guts to have softened Her spirit. She flashes her beam of light so that it dances along the water's crystalline surface, watching, waiting, waiting longer. They are so startled by Her speed and agility, the poor bastards never stand a chance.

"*Bastards* is a bad word," he says.

"Sorry." I think: When you meet the Madwoman in the Sea, you'll understand, too.

This is the tale I tell my son, not only to put him to bed but also as we pace the Diamond Head shoreline, the shallow waters teeming with native coral and fish. He runs his hand through the warm water after I warn him not to, pointing to the red flag flapping just beyond the lifeguard towers, and when the Portuguese man o' war he sifts through his fingers balloons his hand with its venom, I tell him this is the work of the Madwoman in the Sea, punishing the boy who should have listened to his mother, the boy who is simply no good at all.

THE TALE OF the Madwoman in the Sea still startles me even as I hear the words spill over my tongue like bile—*where do I come up with these lies?* We spend half an hour, an hour, every morning, lost in our discourse of the mysterious and atrocious Madwoman, and then an engine outside sputters, and I realize he's missed the bus.

"Fuck," I say. My son tells me I've said a bad word, as if I've never once considered the sound of my own voice. I ignore him, say "fuck" again, softer this time. He waves his arms over his head in giant parabolas. I wedge his too-big feet into his too-tiny sneakers and tug a clean shirt over his head. His hair is feathery, blond and unkempt, like his father's. As are his thin lips, the dimpled arch of his nose, his cleft chin, the freckles peppering his round keiki cheeks. But his eyes are mine, these terrifying gray orbs holding more promise than one could ever hope to live up to. He's certainly a disappointing child, but he's mine, his eyes are mine, I love him dearly.

When we miss the bus, I am responsible. Toby sniffles a little, already resentful of all the ways his friends will cultivate fond memories in his absence, so I am responsible for his distress, just as I am responsible for easing his fears. My son holds entire worlds in his head, dusting off one imaginary catastrophe after another like tugging old books from a shelf. I tell him everything will be okay, an unconvincing argument to raise with a six-year-old. When I fail, I pinch his nose softly, run my thumb along his dimpled chin, smother him with butterfly kisses, call him my strong little warrior, my brave kolohe child. The kolohe, too, he inherited from his father and not from me, though the man is a haole, and probably has no idea what *kolohe* means.

Toby says *kolohe* like a haole—ka-low-hay—so I'm slowly retraining his inherent linguistic ills, pulling his father's spoiled pronunciations from his mouth and dipping him slowly into the cooler, more forgiving waters of ʻōlelo Hawaiʻi, the kānaka maoli tongue. Together we press our palms to our cheeks as we practice elongating our vowels, then lifting the backs of our fingers just under our chins to tighten our *i*'s as we repeat, *lani . . . lani . . . lani . . . lani*, until we're both cackling through our teeth and I've fixed him. It's remarkable, really, the control we have over every unturned stone of our children's potential.

We rally together, me and Toby, because the bus probably reached the school at this point and Toby is poised to receive his third detention slip of the month on account of tardiness, which means I have failed at a fundamental level to provide my son with proper parental care. That's the secret message hidden in the cordially written memo from his private school I can't afford, yet the place I continue depositing him late morning after late morning, a cycle of failures that anchors me, me and Toby both, in its predictable cadence. The detention slip is somewhere in my purse. For some women the contents of their bags are a discreet matter, and they go to great lengths to conceal their cigarettes, their silicone finger vibrators, and all the loose trinkets their spouses advised them not to purchase. Mine is no such bag. Dump it facedown on the floor and all you'll find are those crumpled pink memos detailing my failures as a parent and also a bottle of lorazepam, just a few 100 milligram tablets rattling around the plastic casing.

I chase Toby around the house in a friendly dash to the door, and I think about how my greatest failure is that I willingly stepped into the role of parent in the first place without bothering to ask myself or anyone else around me the simple question, *How do I go on?* I'd assumed going on was just a given, rather than a daily battle ending in punctuating headaches, a dry throat, tears seeping down my face like lazy rivers.

They say the moment you see your baby for the first time makes all the pain and suffering of childbirth worthwhile. After I gave what the doctors called a traumatic birth to Toby, I held him in my arms and loved him instantly, though he resembled an undercooked chicken, all slick and gelatinous and stripped of its beautiful feathers.

The drive from our West Oʻahu compound to his private school in Honolulu is an hour-long expedition through the bleakest junctions of meager living and also a daily reminder of my poor decisions. For the vast sweep of families living on the island's leeward bend, their homes were never a choice. The lilting lānai and sun-bleached exteriors and grime percolating through the wet walls, all this was inherited and no one had any say in the matter. But our story was different, because the moment my husband and I became something, I knew the haole in his blood needed to be diluted, and I was convinced the only way to do so was to rinse it in leeward living. We would be the triumphant melting-pot couple, too good for the comforts of downtown Honolulu. We would buy a shitty plot of arid West Oʻahu land and make it our home.

I was far too young to be married, far too young then to know haole is a stain that never really washes off.

Now my husband is gone, and only me and Toby suffer the consequences of my youthful optimism. We glance out the window and watch the waves unfolding like an old scroll along the waters of Pōkaʻī Bay, and when Toby asks me if She's there, I say yes. We inch to a crawl somewhere along old Farrington Highway, just on the perimeter of a sleepy plantation town where the Waiʻanae Range surges overhead, an eroded backdrop to a history recited only by dead tongues. The traffic plods forward. I pass the time lost in my own head, and Toby passes the time manufacturing fart sounds with his armpit and cupped palm. His best friend, Justin, taught him. Justin's mother, Phoebe, is high-class, a senior account exec at a marketing firm in downtown Honolulu who dons a short, slitted skirt to meet with local celebrities and help them with their image. Toby especially likes her because she feeds the boys homemade banana pudding in these gorgeous crystal chalices after school. Phoebe's saved my ass too many times to count, giving Toby rides and keeping him entertained when I can't get away from my shifts at the hotel. What I can't get past, though, aside from her son's penchant for making his body an instrument of flatulence, is her face's downward cast when I finally retrieve my son, how even when I'm doing everything right, her eyes still blink glassy with condolences.

"For my birthday, I want a big cupcake tower the size of that!" Toby chews the stiff nylon webbing of his seat belt and points to the Waiʻanae Range. I ask him what flavor of enormous cupcake he'd like, and he screams, "TIRAMISU" in my ear.

"You don't even know what tiramisu is," I say, massaging my temples. Every bone and joint in my body is ringing.

"Yeah, I do. Justin had tiramisu for his birthday last month, and that's what I want for mine."

The car ahead of us is a sleek cherry Tesla that roves silently forward. Teslas, what a tacky monstrosity.

I tell him, "Tiramisu has alcohol in it. That's a no-no, remember?"

But he just kicks at the passenger seat until I raise my voice and we both stop talking. In two weeks, Toby will turn seven, which on some days means he will finally stop pissing the bed and I can retire his pull-ups to the closet in the carport, along with the expensive roller skates he's too chicken to try and all his terrible artwork. Mostly it means his father has been gone for three years, and for this absence I have no one to blame but myself. And maybe the Madwoman in the Sea.

I deliver Toby to the school. The moment his feet hit the parking lot pavement, he is off, a heedless little runt infected with the zoomies. He sprints to the outdoor corridor where his pals gather around a towering lattice wall, night-blooming cereus coiling through the wooden panels. Draped over his back is the fraying JanSport bag my own mother bought me when I was in grade school. But Toby was born two months premature, and the bag is a preposterous weight bearing down on his scrawny limbs. My mind scribbles a note: *buy milk*. Milk builds strong bones. Against the lattice, Justin Wong folds over himself to exhibit an impressive handstand, pointing his white Nikes toward the limpid sky. The boys ooh and ahh. One of the little shits pretends to nudge him off balance. Another kid, named Hugh Livingston, bends over and shakes his head of feathery blond hair between his legs. I watch Toby slip a hand through the belted waistline of his uniform khakis and massage his fist in front of his groin, a spastic forward and backward motion that takes me quite some time to recognize as my soon-to-be-seven-year-old son mimicking the act of masturbating. He pretends to jerk off until the bell rings, and the boys laugh and laugh.

HERE'S SOMETHING ELSE you must know about the Madwoman in the Sea: She is too capable to fail. Don't mistake this as a claim of Her perfection, for She is far from perfect. But better than perfection is proficiency, which the Madwoman bears in swells.

"I don't know what *proficiency* is," Toby whines.

I shush him. "Hush now; it's not important."

Her first sighting: under a pier, surging the tide with flicks of Her forked tail. Striped manini and a family of lauʻīpala skim Her pearlescent skin as they glide around Her in loping, concentric rings. She dives underwater and waves to a collection of toxic wana wedged in the shallow reef slope, resting their spindly limbs until the moon surges overhead and they can comb the reef for algae. She passes parrotfish and rays, but She does not spring, knowing full well what She is waiting for.

The first man who finds Her wears rubber flippers and a fool's grin, like nothing bad has ever happened to him. He's snorkeling in a protected marine sanctuary, and with an indelicate hand, he wields a pole for spearfishing, taking infrequent shots and jabs at the pointed kihikihi and resplendent family of uhu ahuʻula, the sheen of their scales suspended like targets in an otherwise muted sea. The man is a hunter; determined, distracted. I don't need to tell you he's a haole. Doesn't see the Madwoman tracking him from behind the blossom of nude finger corals just a few meters off. Stealth, in fact, is just one pillar of Her proficiency, and She springs for him first not with the clutches of Her fingers, or the crack of Her barbed tail, but with Her voice. In a peculiarly elucidated melody, She calls to him underwater, and when he spins around, the man meets Her wicked cuspate grin and Her eyes, all twelve of them fixed and unblinking and famished.

"She's a bad guy," accuses Toby.

Always I am correcting him: She is a woman.

It is at this point in the story when the man negotiates facts. With his fellow spearfishers, his surf buddies, he doesn't like to bring up the instant panic that gripped his belly like a big hand, or the drizzle of piss in his wake. He certainly doesn't mention he swung at the Madwoman with his spear, a measly metal thing, or that with a single swipe of Her hand, the spear was shredded to ribbons. He won't tell them how fast he paddled back to shore, that when he reached the beach, he buried the metal tatters in the sand, that he bought a cheap one from Walmart a week later, because what deplorable piece of shit deserves a market-grade spear?

After the first sighting, the Madwoman develops a taste for obtuse men and their depressive children. She combs through finger corals, weaves in and out of lobe crests teeming with disease as She pursues divers and snorklers with the precision of a marine huntress. Soured by the first man's clumsy escape, She makes a habit of taking something away from the ones who follow. She claws skin cells and stores them under Her sharp nails. Strips them of their rashguard sleeves, a pant leg from their ratty board shorts. From the first child, She shears a thicket of soft fibers tinted blond from years passed under the sun.

With a tight grip, I hold a cluster of Toby's own sun-bleached mop in my hand, pretend to clip it with imaginary finger scissors. He cries into his pillow, leaving a smattering of wet spots on the fabric.

TOBY'S FATHER USED to smile like nothing bad had ever happened to him. It drove me crazy. So one night, after a few glasses of wine, I told Toby's father about the Madwoman in the Sea. It's true I was lolling around the house, my tongue an inflated balloon in my mouth and my better judgment diving into the turbulent sea. His father watched me drink copiously that evening, a sober bystander biding his time until my next inevitable slipup. He was awful that way, always sitting in silent anticipation of my next misstep and smiling. That grin. *I'll show you.*

As for the wine, he refused liquor of all types. Once, I told Toby his father was a teetotaler, for I'd long been fond of the word, and we spent the next two weeks eating dinner around a cheap veneer dining table listening to our three-year-old son recite fabricated words that rhymed with teetotaler.

I'd said, "*Peepolar* is not a word."

His father had said, "Why can't you just play along for once?"

This night in particular was a bad one. Toby'd long fallen asleep among the blankets surging over his trundle bed, and his father and I were alone. We didn't do so well alone anymore. His father cherished quiet, while I was never happy unless I'd kindled something afire. He'd said once that our relationship lacked synergy, but I think we were both just too lonely to spend any meaningful time with each other.

He didn't believe me when I first spoke of the Madwoman. Claimed only a psychopath would concoct a tale so grisly in the hopes of delighting her own child. I did a little dance on my tiptoes and splayed out my arms and said, "Ta-da!" in a way that made him flinch and then admit that he no longer loved me, he *feared* me. I followed him around the house as he prepared for sleep and told him the Madwoman would drown him beneath the weight of her clipped tail, that he'd sink to the ocean floor like a tiny pebble plucked from the shore. I stumbled up the stairs, let something slip between my fingers, shattered my wineglass on the top landing.

"You're just so different," he claimed, collecting the shards of glass into a little pool so that I wouldn't hurt myself. I brought him a plastic trash bag. Kneeling down to help, I hurt myself. The blood made it seem like the stakes had never been so high.

He packed his things a few weeks later. I asked, "What about Toby?" Toby, god, he was still a toddler! Little boys need their fathers.

Toby's father insisted he would continue to be the very best father he could be. It was me he was leaving, not Toby. Yet Toby and I both watched him withdraw from our family with only a small daypack, we peered out from the driveway until not even a blink of his car was left in the distance. For months I harangued him over the phone, insisting we exhaust all our options, we can do this, we can be a family. Here I was, working double shifts at an extravagant resort that serves fleshy, famished tourists swallowed by the elastic of their bathing suits, huddling in the employee bathroom trying to talk sense into my former husband. My son's father. This white man. I told him I would try to be better, but he insisted I was doing everything I could. I had no idea what he meant.

For a while, he called Toby before bed every single night, the unequivocal love of a father. When he stopped calling so frequently, it'd felt somehow like my fault.

I no longer love you, I fear you. Still I loved *him*, his receeding hairline and pockmarked skin and the muted way he moved through the world as though his presence were an inconvenience to be suffered by the poor souls in his path. I loved his exacting scrutiny, and the curious way his jaw would lower ever so slightly when he was concentrating on his research. Toby's father was a mathematician, a life calculated according to the quiet order of numerals. When Toby was born, I'd sneak into the hall late at night to watch his father cradle him in wobbly arms, arms that weren't designed to hold delicate things, arms that sought to accommodate this new reality sprung upon him. The truth was splayed out before me in a rocking chair before I could even name it, certain that none of this would last.

He may have feared me, but what I feared most was the explicit way Toby had embodied his father, and how he looked nothing like me. Their resemblance was uncanny, and for years after his birth, I'd pass long afternoons on the sofa with Toby's paternal grandmother, entertaining her elation as she arranged old photos of Toby's father on the coffee table, plucked an arbitrary print as though she'd just won the lottery, wielded the thing intimately in my face as she claimed their impossible likeness. As if I didn't already know. As if I didn't lie beside the identical twins each night, considering their every wrinkle and cleft chin and blossom of freckles and all their light hair. She was immensely proud, and I was a mother to a hapa-haole son with a haole husband living in the shambles of leeward Oʻahu, where everyone assumed we were in the military. Just another white couple cultivating roots on Hawaiian land.

So maybe Toby's father and I didn't love our son in the same way. But the worst part of it all was his father's abject refusal to acknowledge how sorely I *did* love him, how when Toby was born premature I cried for twenty hours straight, begging the night nurse not to stow him away in some plastic box, begging her to keep him nestled here in my arms, sobbing and shriveled and safe, with me.

But the night nurse, she took him. Locked him away in the NICU, then when I screamed sedated me with a significant dose of morphine. I relaxed. His father drove fifteen miles west to spend the night in our home rather than crunched in a disfigured recliner beside my hospital bed. Toby wilted away in the tundra of the NICU. Amid the midnight purr and whirl of persistent hospital monitors, I flipped through the same twelve channels on the television and watched beautiful, elegant white people dance and eat and cook and fall in love. A handsome stranger held a woman by her waist as he puffed on a cigar. A chef dutifully narrated the trick to julienne a carrot, then invited someone from the live audience to come onstage and practice. Her blade turned on its side resembled the surface of the ocean where, submerged, something unborn and truly heinous murmurs. If Toby lives, I'd told myself, I will teach my son not to fear the ocean. I will teach him to think audacious thoughts and act with insolence. It doesn't help to move through the world with timorous steps. If my son lives, he will not be a numbers boy. I will paddle him to the outside breaks and show him what it's like to swim for your life.

Toby's father is a good man, perhaps a better man than our son will be. He may have left, but he left me the house, his car, the quilted bedspread I adored, a freezer full of prepared meals, our son. On weekends when it was his turn to father, he taught Toby how to recover from a toppled bike, taught him how to hold a knife while curling his fingers around the skin of a cucumber to avoid slicing off his hand. He supervised soccer games and chauffered him to and from preschool classes. In the first months of Toby's life, our baby secured firmly in the back seat of the car, he circled the perimeter of our tiny island for hours and hours, if only to show our son what it meant to attend to a world stained with luminescence, a world that glows.

What, then, ultimately drives a good man away from his family? Not power or fame, lust or cowardice, ennui or opportunity. A Madwoman, that's who.

★ ★ ★

THE SON I bore prances through the house like a stotting gazelle, weaving around tables, desks, floor lamps, chairs, stools, swelling the space with the charisma uniquely possessed by a six-going-on-seven-year-old. A fetus. Nothing more than gaunt bones and a clumsy spring in his step. I curl my fingers around the perspiring neck of a Kirin, and when I ask Toby where he learned to make that motion, the one with his hand moving up and down in his pants, he lies.

"The Madwoman," he insists. "She showed me how."

I feel the tops of my ears bloom a fiery red like the tip of an iron poker. This curious rage, it always manifests itself in the strangest of places. "That's not true, Tobs. Remember what I told you about little boys who lie?"

"The Madwoman gets them."

The bottle I'm clutching feels smooth along its feminine contours, and when I peel my fingers from the glass, drops of condensation prickle my lap. I blink hard, and when I open my eyes, Toby has cornered a baby moth behind the end table, his tiny hands poised to attack.

"Don't!" I shriek.

He stares at me bug-eyed, as though I've misplaced my manners, or my mind.

"Remember what I told you? We don't kill moths in this house."

"Why not? They're bugs." Then his whole face crunches inward. "They're *disgusting*."

"They're our *ancestors*. This is how your grandparents and great-grandparents and everyone who came before you pays us a visit."

"Gross!" Now his whole face is a plane of punctured tin. "I don't care."

He slaps at the wall but is too slow, and the moth flies skyward, ascending to a higher perch.

Toby whimpers and moans; I hold him in my arms until we're both shaking.

Then Toby is whining for dinner, and the kitchen is the only room in which I am needed. My hands go weeding through the refrigerator, searching for food I haven't let spoil. Toby sits cross-legged on the floor then springs around again, making those hand-underarm fart sounds, and I don't understand him, don't know how to talk to him. Perhaps it's normal for kids to lie and sprint and pretend to jerk off in front of their friends, and I am simply too antiquated to meet him halfway. Perhaps it's as his father said, *Why can't you just play along for once?* I flip frozen veggie patties bitten by frost on their crisp ends, the hibachi drafting thick fumes through the kitchen, the living room. The smoke detector deploys, a resounding clamor that quiets only when I drag our table fan into the kitchen and cast its rotating blades toward the alarm. Fucking piece-of-shit technology, stupid goddamn house. Toby presses his palms to his ears and grimaces. The alarm stops. I think about how I insisted we move here, the tenements of leeward Oʻahu seductive in their strange deformities. Years later and still I was learning proximity to the slums and the sea would in no way imbue the men I loved most with the kuleana of my own ancestry; no matter where we dropped our anchor, Toby would always be hapa, just as his father would always be haole. Three different people, and none of us really belonging here.

We settle in for dinner. I spoon wilted steamed spinach and a heap of white rice and a burnt veggie burger on a paper plate and sprinkle the dish with a few shriveled carrot sticks. I eat my veggie burger slathered in ketchup and mayonnaise and listen to Toby brag about the mango sticky rice Phoebe Wong served the boys today after school, and I pierce a carrot stick with the tines of my fork and think, *Goddamn sea witch, goddamn ocean cunt*. I stare at Toby and the braid of spinach unfurling over his bottom lip. Soon he will grow older and massage gel in his hair and his old shoes will compress his feet and his pants will sag past his taut hips. Observing friends like Justin Wong and Hugh Livingstone, he will cultivate a new and foreign language that's bound to clash with my own grasp of speech, and we will argue. We'll argue about curfews and girls and grades and his gross inability to wipe scum from the surface of our dishware, and eventually he, too, will no longer love me, he'll *fear* me, and then I'll be alone again.

I think, *As it should be.*

Also, *I am afraid.*

For dessert, I hand him a pint of his favorite rocky-road ice cream and a clean spoon and encourage him to go to town. Together we curl up on the sofa, and I lay a soft Hawaiian quilt over Toby's lap and knit a tress of his whispy hair between my fingers while an old Jason Bourne film animates from the television. For a while I proposed Pixar movies, shows on the Disney Channel, *PAW Patrol*, and that Irish animated series with the child veteranarian who nurses anthropomorphic toys. None of it took. But Matt Damon scaling buildings as a CIA assassin riddled with amnesia? This shit captivates Toby like nothing else.

I drift off slowly, one finger spun around my son's soft curls. Still drinking from a sippy cup, Toby reclines his head against my rib cage, compressing into all the doughy parts I haven't bothered to condition since well before his father left. I kiss the tiny swirl at the top of his head, kiss his fluttery little eyelashes. My perfect, sweet, awful, hapa, kolohe little boy. He clings both hands around his sippy cup, yet I feel the weight of his arms cinch all around me, collapsing into me, and it is a beautiful and bloodcurdling weight that sinks me into slumber.

ANOTHER CONVERSATION BETWEEN a mother and son:
    Setting: the car.
    Temperature: 91 degrees, 120 percent humidity.

Mood: tepid, with hints of significant room for improvement.

Topic: preferred guests to attend a seventh birthday, and also cookies.

"But I had cookies last week in the morning at Justin's!" he cries, hurling his boy feet against the back of the passenger's seat. *Thump*, and again.

"You cut that out," she snaps. "And I don't care if you had them before, it's too early for cookies. Period. Now let's think about your party for a minute. Do you know which of the kids from school you want to invite?"

"I want lemon wafers."

"I don't care. Answer my question."

He huffs. "I dunno. I guess Justin and Hugh, and Kepa and Ryder and maybe Lopaka, but he was sorta making fun of me yesterday."

"About what?"

"Not knowing how to swim. He said only haoles and popolos can't swim."

She sucks air through her teeth. "I don't want you saying those words, Tobs. I told you that before."

"Sorry. I forgot."

"I mean *popolo*. Don't use that word, with your friends or with me. *Haole* is whatever."

"I said I'm *sorry*."

"And that's not even true. Shit." She flicks on her left blinker, maneuvers a quick U-turn.

"That's a bad word," he says softly.

She sighs. "Sorry. But wait, can we go back to the swimming thing? You want to learn how to swim? I thought you were afraid of the ocean."

"I'm not afraid of nothing." He crosses his arms.

"I can teach you, you know."

"I don't want you, I want swimming class."

"I'm a really good swimmer—"

"Kainoa and Justin and Ryder all take swimming class together. They get to go for shave ice after, too. It's a friend thing."

She chuckles. "Well, if it's a *friend thing*. Though who knows how much this friend thing is gonna cost—oh *shit*." She crushes her foot against the brake pedal, the car squealing to a steady crawl.

"That's a bad word."

"*Sorry*. No one knows how to drive in this goddamn city. Baby, this is why we live where we live, okay?"

"I like the city. Justin has a koi pond in his front yard. And Hugh has a pool."

"Why should that matter? You don't even know how to swim."

WHEN I REALLY want to freak out my son, I tell him something else legend claims: the Madwoman takes the first child when his back is turned to the water. It's the worst mistake you can make when you're submerged waist-deep in an ecosystem that doesn't belong to you.

But the boy is tender, no shining paragons of parenthood to speak of. He learns mostly by observing others, and when a fellow keiki rolling around in the shallows faces the shoreline, the boy turns to follow suit.

Just a few seconds. The Madwoman in the Sea needs only a few seconds to execute Her ploy, which really is one of power. It is power that propels Her forward, through surging currents that initially restrain Her, inhibit Her charge toward the unsuspecting boy until Her resistance is too much to bear and the waves see Her for who She really is—a crazy fucking madwoman who will always get what she wants.

Toby is livid. "That's a *really* bad word!"

I smooth out his baby hairs and shush him.

As She approaches the boy, the water undulates choppily, and a steady hum of sound lapses through the current—the tune that drew the first man to Her, a rousing melody the boy is too young to deem a danger. In fact, the sound reminds him of his grandmother, and the songs she would sing to him late at night while crouched over his bedside. Before she died. This is what the boy is thinking about when his ankle is held hostage by the barbed clutches of something mysterious, something he cannot see.

Suddenly, the boy is overturned. A strong undercurrent flips him on his back and something is still clutching his ankle, something heinous, as he scuffles with the formless water and all its fury. For seconds his nostrils surface, then are tugged back down into the waterworld along with his flailing arms, kicking legs, tufts of unwashed hair, pelvis that pulses almost intuitively to the strange and subdued melody. He doesn't think, doesn't really see Her until he does.

The tail, a venomous serpent studded with millions of tiny blades; twelve eyes peering into his own eyes and soul and gut.

There's no time to sound any alarms, and anyway, the boy has no parents who truly love him in a profound, maddening way, who will give rise to his salvation. *Just a few more seconds*, he thinks, kicking his legs furiously in an impossible dash to the translucent ceiling of water that is within reach, for he can see it! The soft shimmer of a world that appeared mostly dull and decayed for the few years he spent trampling it until now. *Just a few more seconds*, he thinks with each futile kick. *A few more seconds until I can breathe again, until I can save myself.*

The Madwoman in the Sea cackles, a sound that bears no difference to the rousing melody—it is the only sound She knows.

When I cackle, my son wraps one hand over my mouth and tells me to hush, because I'm upsetting him.

SURE, THE DIAMOND Head waters are all good and fine for frolicking, and no one ever turned up their nose to an afternoon submerged in the familiar warmth of

Waikīkī Beach, but teaching a child how to swim requires a tranquil privacy one can find only on the North Shore, so this is where we go.

The drive over, and Toby seems excited, if slightly anxious. He wears his inflated arm floaties as accessories even though I've reminded him floatation devices will not be allowed once we enter the water, and he keeps cracking his jaw, unhinging his lips as he opens and closes his mouth to the distractive rhythmic clicking while we drive in otherwise silence. It's a curious habit, and while I'm certain the violent act itself cannot be good for his oral health, I say nothing. I change lanes and think of how Toby's father no longer loves me, he *fears* me, even though I'm the one sticking around long enough to teach our hapa child how to swim for his life. This child who doesn't even *look like me*, who may not even enjoy my company as much as he enjoys his absent father's. We take the H-2, weaving through forest beds of acacia and canopies of persimmon trees that blur as an emerald sweep through the glass of the speeding car. When we reach Waialua, the towering acacias give way to the subdued graves of former sugarcane and pineapple plantations, now long-fallow fields in the clutches of wealthy developers and gentleman's farm estates. Behind the fields, the backside of the eroded Wai'anae Range rises up to greet us.

I point out the mountain range, explaining that our home is situated on the foothills just over and beyond the tall summit. But Toby isn't listening. He sucks on the seat belt's stiff nylon and gapes at his feet dangling from the booster. There is no way to relieve his fear of the ocean without seeing him as a small child I adore deep in my gut and therefore am inclined to protect, so I continue driving the Kam Highway bend through Kahuku until the turquoise bowl of Kawela Bay looms westward in our window and I pull over and park along the side of the road.

Jostling a child in and out of a car and then across a single-lane highway burdened with intermittent traffic is no easy feat. Like always, I do my best, and under the bristling heat of late fall we successfully navigate the highway barrier and all we lose is an arm float.

"Forget it," I tell him on the beach as we collect our slippers to walk through the sand. "We won't need floaties anyway. We're gonna be big kids and stay afloat on our own, right?"

Toby nods then scampers away, spellbound in a vigorous state that emerges only when broiling humidity meets the boundless expanse of softened North Shore sand. The break I've chosen is neither crowded nor well known; it is a private lull in the chaos of tourism and crowds that soothes my soul just padding along the springy carpet of sand. Freed from the constraints of the floaties and the car seat, Toby is delighted. I chase him in careening circles while we kick up debris behind our heels and collapse in a cushioned bed of wet sand. Foamy whitewater laps at our splayed legs, and Toby bounds away. A thin scar like a winding loop of string is still stitched across his left palm from his encounter with the Portuguese man o' war, but I don't feel sorry for him. I watch him draw organic shapes in the sand with his little kid toes and mostly feel like I will never again experience this moment, how as soon as I print it in my mind, the material, corporeal thing has already passed, and how curiously sad this discovery weighs on me.

"You ready, bud?" I ask, brushing sand from my knees and peeling my shorts over my hips. Tube of sunscreen in my hand, and Toby wears me down with his ceaseless sprinting away, the flutter in his youthful steps and the breezy way he meanders the shoreline with no acknowledgment of my continual efforts to safeguard his life. I shake my head, yank him by the hem of his board shorts. "Melanoma, do you want melanoma?" I scream, though of course he doesn't understand the question. He crumples into a little bug ball on the sand. He says my name—Mom—over and over again: "Mom, I'm a little bug ball! Uh itty-bitty bug ball! I'm a bug ball, Mom!" I bite the swollen insides of my cheeks and say, "Nice job, buddy, really nice job."

Once submerged in the chilly water, though, neither of us is a little bug ball, and especially not Toby, who flounders easily, complains incessantly of exhaustion and heatstroke even though I'm the one kicking my legs furiously to keep us afloat and also he doesn't know what heatstroke is—probably another life lesson from Justin Wong. I let the current, stronger than I'd expected on such a windless day, steer us where it wills, for there is no rush, we both have so much time. Toby braids his fingers together and wraps them around my neck with force. I tell him, "Ow, Tobs, lighter touch, please. That hurts." A slight draft drifts us shoreward, and Toby clings tighter. I feel the bruises bloom along my neck without witnessing the injury firsthand, which is the best way I can describe being a mother.

"Water's cold, Mama. It's too cold." Along with his fingers, Toby's legs wrap my waist like tentacles. I flutter my arms through the water and kick my feet, and somehow we stay upright, me and my son. "It's cold and I *hate* this. I don't, really don't wanna do it." Toby starts to groan.

"Don't worry, bud. You're fine. We're fine. It's cold now, but it'll get warmer, okay?"

Toby asks, "Are we swimming?"

I say, "Not yet."

"How do you know when you're swimming?"

I tell him he's swimming when he can kick his feet and move his arms and stay afloat without my help. He scrunches his nose, and a lick of saltwater laps at his face.

"I got water in my nose!" he shrieks. His hold on my neck slackens, and he bolts upright as if jolted from a terrible nightmare. It confounds me, this clench of panic while bathing in the plenary bliss of the mountains and the sea. Then again, he is his father's son. Identical as printer copies.

I take great care to carry him farther through the ocean without triggering his attention; it's the only way we'll make it anywhere, really. We move as one unit over soft, undulating waves, the whitewater hissing its descent behind us.

"You ready to practice swimming?" I ask him, and over and over again, his answer is no.

"You know I'm not gonna let anything bad happen to you. All you need to do is let go and practice doggy paddling. Remember how we practice in the tub? Kick your legs and move your arms back and forth, like you're dancing. You'll be fine."

A strong, briny mist burrows its way through our nostrils, and a wave careens then breaks just a few feet away from our bobbing bodies. Toby stiffens.

"I wanna go back," he says, quietly at first, a near whisper, and then again, louder and much louder. "I wanna go back, I wanna go back to the beach. I don't wanna do this, I wanna go back." Never, not once, does he say *please*.

I don't know why this omission tunnels fury through my blood.

I think, *My stubborn, lazy, kolohe, pathetic little child. How did I ever tolerate you?* I think his existence is the only thing that anchors my feet to the ground every morning. His fingers are claws penetrating my neck, but then it is me with the cuspate teeth, me with the twelve eyes and tanned skin and forked razor tail and all the spiraled seaweed hair floating around us like a veil. Just as it is my curious melody that catches him in the snarls of my trap, the tune that reassures him over and over again: *Everything will be fine, you can trust me, I'm not gonna let anything bad happen to you, I promise.* His muscles relax, his grip goes limp.

I release him.

But something about his attempt to swim is faulty, though I can't distinguish a single point of error; rather, it's more a cluster of misguided motions that beat the energy from his baby bones yet tug him downward, downward toward the chilly and unnavigable ocean floor. His hands and legs jerk sporadically as though gripped by a seizure, and flecks of saltwater splash me in the face. The brine webs my eyes ruby red. I think, *We are most beautiful here, where no one can see us and no one can ever, ever find us.*

Then Toby's moppy blond hair emerges from the water, his nostrils and pruned lips surface, and he spouts cries, pleas, promises, apologies, lies. He begs me to help him. But I am helping him, I tell myself as I wade a few paces back, my arms and legs pulsing naturally, like magic. I'm helping him swim for his life, and this is the only way either of us will ever learn.

Just a few more seconds, buddy, I tell him this tale until I, myself, believe it. Just a few more seconds and you'll be swimming just like me.

Ms. Amelia's Salon for Women in Charge

Kehaulani never minded her pubic hair, so when the salons first started showing up across Oʻahu, she felt no impulse to throng the doors, join the snaking lines of snakelike women who waited ravenous, relentless, desperate for their next wax.

It was Bennett who convinced her otherwise.

Now she has assumed the mask of a Different Person: a person who waxes. She cannot afford a monthly pass; she makes up for the wide swaths of time between appointments with hydrating shaving cream and a razor. Four blades, and still the bumps rise to the surface of her skin like tiny volcanoes fixing to erupt. She copes and cancels dates with Bennett—she is ashamed to be seen with a skin rash so vulgar she can't romp around her own apartment in just her underwear. Bennett offers to front her the money.

But *offers* isn't right—that boy *begs*.

But Kehaulani would like to try doing things on her own, which is why she has endured a five-month waiting list before driving halfway across the island to visit the highly lauded Ms. Amelia's Salon for Women in Charge. She circles the bustling parking lot twice before finding a compact stall where pigeons peck at an abandoned Spam musubi and what might pass as an egg-salad sandwich. The smell is wretched; she holds her breath. She follows the neon glow of the entrance sign like it contains a fortune or her most promising future.

The locked door fences her adrenaline. She pauses, reads the sign on the door that instructs her to please be patient, for they are at the moment servicing a record number of clients. The waiting room is currently at capacity, but she is welcome to use any number of benches lining the exterior entrance. A certified wax specialist will be with her shortly.

Kehau peers through the glass doors, the walls made of glass, but the tinting is dramatic, and all she sees is her own ugly outline. She sits on one of the benches. She sits in the swamp of her own sweat, sunlight pooling in from the pale skies above. A call to Bennett would be a fine way to fill the time. Or a call to her mother. She was once so close to her mother, but now they haven't spoken in months, and Kehau is anxious to make contact. Instead she fills the time with urban sounds: car honks, tires screeching to brake, the whistling of sliding doors opening and closing to the mall next door. The four-hundred dollars she is saving by waxing at Ms. Amelia's is ripe in her mind. As is her vagina, beige and hairless and supposedly pretty as a flower that way.

She waits a good ten minutes before a delicate bell chimes at the doorway, and a woman calls her name. *Key-how-lan-y?* The woman is haole, clearly from nowhere near here, and somehow Kehau can't even score a job temping at the Xerox inside this very mall. The haole receptionist is also beautifully overweight, with overly powdered cheeks and a coal-black uniform with red stitching near the breast that reads *Ms. Amelia's*. She smiles theatrically, as if sincerity has no place in this manufactured world.

The woman ushers Kehau into the lobby, where the cool A/C laps at her face and framed portraits of slender, bikini'd wāhine gaze down on her. She follows the receptionist to the fuchsia counter that shines liquid smooth under the champagne lights. Curiously pastoral music plays through speakers Kehau cannot see; it lends the impression that she is awaiting a luxurious spa experience. She is used to salon receptionists asking for prepayment in full and for said prepayment to total hundreds of dollars. Instead, the woman cheerily declares a zero-sum amount, but not before reminding Kehau of her choice, which must be decided upon before she leaves Ms. Amelia's for the day.

"Your wax specialist will be with you shortly!"

Kehau nods then takes a seat on a sticky pleather bench, identical to the set outside but warmer somehow, despite the pleasant indoor weather of the place. She doesn't know how to quantify *shortly* in her mind. She texts Bennett, to remind him that in just a few hours, he will be pau with work and she will be waiting for him, in bed and naked and smooth as an eggshell.

She is pleased with herself, sincerely, a rarity for this point in her life and her relationship. She thinks fondly of Bennett, whom she met two years prior on a dating app. Bennett was objectively dull, a "banker" by trade, but expressed his interest in a way that pared open Kehau's thighs and heart, making up a bed for him. Never did he ask her to wax directly, though he balked at her razor rash when first making its acquaintance, his face collapsing inward like punched dough. Six months into their relationship, Kehau resolved to rid at least her bikini line of springy pubic hairs (she found a Groupon for a half-priced wax), and goodness, the look on Bennett's face when they reunited post-wax. You would've thought she'd returned from Vegas thousands of dollars richer! Now Kehau looks forward to that face, counts down the days on a pink pocket calendar when his superficial glee might poke its head out from the sand and smile.

"Oh, honey, before I forget." The receptionist leans over the counter to hand Kehau a series of forms clamped to a clipboard. "We'll need your signature on these, and if you flip to the back page, you'll find a list of options for your trait exchange. Just look these over and let me know if you have any questions."

Kehau combs through the paperwork. The first is a consent form permitting Ms. Amelia's Salon to collect Kehau's selected personality trait in exchange for her bikini wax. She signs after barely skimming the fine print; fastidiousness was never a trait she could boast of. The final form contains an extremely comprehensive list of potential traits for clients' consideration. Agreeable, confident, courteous, creative, eloquent, fun, generous, idealistic, intuitive, loyal, methodical, open, optimistic, resourceful, spontaneous, tolerant. So many options, and how is a woman to choose?

She doesn't. Not this instant, and not without another woman pushing down on her, pressuring her to decide and to act. She passes the forms back to the receptionist, all information submitted, excluding the selected trait. She would like to ask the woman how one scores a job at a prominent salon such as Ms. Amelia's, but then the phone is ringing, and the woman's attention is drawn elsewhere. Concurrently, Kehau's phone buzzes in her lap. She reads the screen, dim and smudged with her own faint fingerprints:

Can't wait, baby!

And an aggregation of emojis whose narrative is impossible to discern.

Should she return to her apartment still furrowed with pubic hair and the entire amalgam of her personality intact, what would Bennett think? How might his sculptured face fall, and how sorely might his disappointment disappoint her? Since losing her job and thereby her source of reliable income, Kehau has noticed the small yet significant ways in which she has bent her will to the will of Bennett, restructured her person to accommodate what he desires of her. In the beginning, her acquiescence did not bother her. She even gladly suffered his shameful Caucasian faux pas—correcting her pronunciation in front of others, and planting his chopsticks in a mound of white rice. Things that would make her mother shudder, she tolerated. So long as he continued to front her rent money, so long as he treated her to meals and to movies. Only after her third flop of a job interview—this one manning the phone for a midlevel town dentist, for god's sake—did apprehension creep to the surface of her psyche. Submission was fine but unsustainable. Soon Bennett will tire of her, as all men have, and even her smooth, hairless vagina will prove insignificant.

She should enjoy the pleasure while it lasts, for it never lasts long.

A tinctured voice calls her name. Kehaulani looks up and meets the gaze of a grinning woman, so petite, strikingly beautiful. All Kehau's prior thoughts are dwarfed by the woman's shrill tone, her kindly manner that is so kind it approaches insincere. Her shiny black hair, sharply trimmed, meets her protruding collarbones, and although she wears the same coal uniform as the receptionist, Kehau notices a difference in the pink stitching, an absence of the apostrophe and the *s*.

"My name is Ms. Amelia, and I'm so excited to be servicing you today."

Kehaulani's breath catches near the base of her throat. She cannot wait to tell Bennett that she was serviced by Ms. Amelia—*the* Ms. Amelia—who guides her now down a wide, fluorescent hall and into the second room on the left. A click of the door, then of a lock.

She asks as though resuming a conversation: "And remind me when your last wax was?"

Unthinkingly, or perhaps thinking too much, Kehau lies. Three months.

Ms. Amelia sucks air through her teeth, then tsks. "Long time to go without, honey."

Kehau nods, appraising the room that will deliver her into hairlessness. Here the walls are dressed in floral etchings and more prints of beachy women, all tanned and glorious with their artificial grins and pristine bikini lines. They arch their backs, display a series of confident poses, and betray none of the traits they've forfeited for such persistently smooth skin.

"It was becoming expensive," Kehau tries to explain. "I'm really grateful to've gotten an appointment here."

"Of course! Beauty is pain and all that. I can tell you more about our loyalty program if you like, once we're done here."

Kehau grins. "I'd like that." She prepares for the worst of the experience, which is undressing in front of a stranger. She gets it over with quickly, unrolls her shorts over her wide hips and her underwear, too, a beige cotton dumpster. She pockets the clothing in her purse, which dangles from a chrome hook beside the door, then climbs onto the reclined spa bed, the draped tissue paper splintering under her weight.

"We're doing the full Brazilian today?" Ms. Amelia asks, standing over a giant cauldron of wax.

Kehau nods, contracting her legs into butterfly position where she feels her vagina peel open like a clamshell.

"And do we know what trait we're trading in?"

Kehau doesn't respond. The artificial air pulsing through the vents licks at her vagina, and it's hard to think of anything but being splayed out on that bed like meat prepared for butchering.

"I . . . haven't decided yet," she admits. Before leaving his place two nights ago, Kehau had reminded Bennett of the appointment while trying to push her arm through the elusive left sleeve of her blouse. He was drinking red wine from a stemless glass, and he didn't offer to help her. Instead, he encouraged her to choose a trait whose loss might make her gainfully employable.

She didn't tell her mother she'd capitulated to one of *those* salons. No matter their prolonged silence; she loves her mother dearly and knows well enough the woman would not approve.

"I can just get started and give you some time to think, though we'll need your decision before checking you out of here. Wax temp okay?"

Kehau didn't even feel the first brush of wax along her inner thigh, hadn't felt anything at all, really, except cold and swampy, lying there with all that sweat clogging the lanes of her pubic hair. But now that Ms. Amelia has given occasion to the wax, Kehau feels it—the immediacy of the warm glop as it meets her inner thigh. The damp, balmy thrill of it. She nods, the wax temp is perfect.

Ms. Amelia's fingers fold over her left thigh, the sturdy meat of it, and it's a touch that pearls moisture from Kehau's forehead.

"You ready, honey?" But before Kehau can answer, Ms. Amelia is yanking the strip of solidified wax from Kehau's tender skin. Pain beetles through her thighs, climbs the crenellations of her spine, swims through the bends in her brain. Her hands crunch into tiny fists. Then, a wash of nothing. It is survivable, and more than that, it is pleasure.

"You're doing great. Skin's looking just fine, too. How long did you say it's been since your last wax?"

Kehau takes a breath, the tissue paper puckering under her. "About three months," she lies again, because three is a smooth number while eight is a weight in her mouth.

"Auwē, so long! It's amazing your skin's held up so well. Long, coarse hairs help."

"Okinawan hair problems," she jokes, but Ms. Amelia only stares, makes a mess of a smile.

Another layer of hot wax brushes over her pelvis, this time scraping against the wet lip of her labia. A hazard of the practice, and Ms. Amelia apologizes, but Kehau only waves her off. Heat spindles through her pelvis. She imagines the wax cooling, burnished, drying over her body like clay panels.

An idea, then. Kehau lifts her head from the cushioned pad.

"How exactly do you get a job as a waxer?" she asks. "I've been looking for work for some time."

"We're wax *specialists*," Ms. Amelia clarifies. "And it's a rather long process. We've got one hell of a waiting list."

"What about working reception? Or I could do some sort of janitorial thing for a while until a spot opens up—"

"You're mighty eager, huh?"

She takes a long time applying the next layer to Kehau's skin.

Kehau closes her eyes, lets the warmth of the wax fold over her and relaxes her mind. She is so tired; mining for work is exhausting. During her last job interview, this one for a sales job at the Kakaʻako Rice Factory, a kindly Japanese grandma asked Kehau if she could identify her best three qualities. In her response, Kehau didn't stumble. She had rehearsed this response for the duration of her unemployment. Now, with the whole ensemble of her personality in question, Kehau struggles to identify which traits she's meant to safeguard, which ones are essential to her person.

Alas, they all are. And isn't that the point of this currency?

Easing into the next wax strip, Kehau would like to explain to Ms. Amelia how she didn't get the Rice Factory job, or the job at the printing shop, or the receptionist job at the dentist's, or the barista job or the real estate job or the cashier job at Longs. She has considered signing with Uber or Lyft, but her car isn't reliable, while gas prices are exorbitant. She spent a few months on TaskRabbit but made less than minimum wage during ten-hour shifts. She is rapidly approaching thirty and still Kehau hasn't made a dent in her college loans, her monthly car payments, all the bills. If she could find a job, temp somewhere, even, then perhaps she could entertain the possibility of leaving Bennett. But of course she would never leave Bennett! Her emergency contact, her most sincere love. Her friends have called him forgettable, but it's Bennett she is always thinking about, and while she braces for the searing pain of the last wax strip, she thinks of Bennett, whose favorite food is fried pickles and anything soured by time. His arm hairs are so fair they look covered in gloss. Nothing has soothed her more than petting Bennett's wispy blond hairs while his body curls around her in her tiny twin bed. How different her life would be, she thinks, with a job. Without Bennett.

For as long as she can remember, Kehaulani has sought to behave in ways that run parallel to her intuition, her long-held beliefs. Her principles and her naʻau. She would like to think she has always been a genuine, sincere, resolute person. But she still can't bring herself to call her mom, and the choice of which trait to isolate, which trait to renounce, weighs heavy in her hands. She imagines there is a way for things to be easier. She imagines her vagina as hairless and gleaming.

And then the wax is over, pau. Ms. Amelia rubs Kehau's nude pelvis with post-waxing serum and an ivory cloth towel. She recites boilerplate language about the recovery process: "You'll be red and sore for a while, and don't forget to wait a few days before exfoliating, and remember to use your serum! Your minimizing lotion! Remember to wait twenty-four hours before having sex or going to the beach so that your follicles can close . . ."

What she really wants to know is which trait Kehaulani is prepared to renounce in exchange for this phenomenal waxing experience.

"I'm sorry," Kehau says quietly. "I haven't decided yet."

She slinks off the bed, waddles over to her bag and her clothes, waits for Ms. Amelia to offer some advice. But this is a business, and this is not Ms. Amelia's job, her job is complete.

"Look, the thing is, I can't let you leave here without making a choice."

Kehau nudges her shorts around her fold of belly.

"What would you pick?" she asks, buttoning the little cuff of denim.

"I can't answer that for you, honey."

"I don't mean what you think I should pick. I really want to know what you'd be willing to give up."

Ms. Amelia holds a tablet to her chest. After some time passes, she answers the question—says, "You'll be done with it and no one will ever know the difference"; says, "It frees you"—and Kehau agrees. She would very much like to be freed. From Bennett, from financial strain, from her mother. Ms. Amelia enters Kehau's response into the tablet then guides her to the lobby. The former receptionist has been replaced by a big-bellied hapa beauty, a young girl with apricot-blushed cheeks who looks like Kehau. She skims through her paperwork for the currency Kehau is meant to exchange. Rattles away on her keyboard. Something shutters inside Kehau, this sense of a flattened self, and then it is finished. The receptionist says Ms. Amelia would like to see her again in four weeks for her next wax, and you'd better believe Kehau makes that appointment knowing full well she won't show up. Bennett, she thinks, will be so pleased. He'll bring his hands over every inch of her skin and feel nothing but roils of pleasure. She'll say her perfectionist tendencies are gone, and she will never tell him what she really chose to give up in its place. She thanks the receptionist then strolls out of Ms. Amelia's Salon for Women in Charge as though sincerity means nothing to her, because finally, it does.

Hotel Molokai

We were in the air for no more than fifteen minutes when our seats started to quake, and the pilot announced our impending descent into Kaunakakai, Molokai. Through the plane's distorted PA system, she asked the flight attendants to please prepare the cabin for landing, but this wasn't a cabin, and I hadn't gotten settled enough in the few minutes we'd spent aloft to warrant preparation for any impending discomfort. My tray table stuck out like a swollen tongue, broken. These seats didn't even recline.

Our aircraft was a commuter Cessna that sat nine people uncomfortably and soared through the air with its wings splayed out like a woman's feet in stirrups, preparing to give birth. Along with me, there was my grams, with whom I was flying, a haole couple on their honeymoon, and a preposterously old white man named Alvin. Alvin was a birder. He sat in the row behind me, flipping through a native-bird identification guide and occasionally reaching forward to tap my shoulder and inquire after the pronunciation of a particular species.

Through the tiny oval window, I could see the plane's propellers rotate ecstatically to keep us suspended above the sea. I glanced down, and we were so close to shore, I could watch the seafoam accumulate in cottony pulls along the Pacific's glistening surface, the infrequent cherry buoy bobbing with the current. In the seat across the aisle, Grams was filing her fingernails. It was a strange obsession of hers, this meticulous attention to the healthy sheen of her nails, and while I hadn't noticed it before personally, I had amassed enough of my mother's dull grievances leading up to this trip to prepare myself for, among other curiosities, ample nail filing. Grams held her bubblegum-pink filer in her left hand, glanced up at me, and smiled.

As turbulence thundered through the Cessna's womb, one of two Filipino flight attendants, this one a jeweled māhū with an enormous ass, strutted through the aisle cradling a shallow paper box. The flight wasn't long enough to warrant an industrial food and beverage cart, nor were the aisles wide enough to accommodate one. Instead, the attendant reached into his box, from which he dispensed dimpled plastic cups of Passion Orange Guava, recently chilled for our consumption. I took a cup. The theatrics he displayed in this simple gesture reminded me of a magician pulling colorful ribbons from his black top hat, though I had never seen a magician perform such an act in my life. I had never seen a magician, period.

While the plane shuddered and stirred, the propellers shrieking as if they'd been set on fire, I tore open the drink's foil top and brought it to my lips. Sweet, pulpy orange mingled with the tart acidity of ripened guava. It tasted like my hale, like my mother. She was so far away and yet always I considered her in every choice I made, from the moment I boarded this stupid plane until she would retrieve me from the HNL baggage claim three days later. In my adult years, I'd blush with shame at my unhealthy display of separation anxiety, this insecure attachment to my mother I'd cultivated well into my teens. But at the time of the trip, my first venture across the Pacific without her, all I managed to do was miss her acutely.

The senior birder behind me gulped his juice loudly, smacked his errant and veiny lips. The sounds he made were terrible. He guffawed and hummed; he clicked his tongue as he read. Even the pages of his bird guide made an awful peeling sound when he turned them. I tried to be kind. I didn't even laugh at his horrendous pronunciation of ʻōlelo Hawaiʻi. The māhū flight attendant returned to encourage us all to buckle up, and something squeezed my shoulder. It was the man's decrepit hand, wrinkled beyond recognition, tints of blue veins running rivulets beneath his white, white skin. I strained to make eye contact, and he wedged through the split between seats his native bird guide, turned to a page about 'apapane. I'd seen the crimson honeycreeper several times in my life, usually while hiking Makiki Loop with Mom. It was a stupefyingly simple bird, as common as a wailing mynah, or a nasty street pigeon.

"Ah-pah-PAH-neh," I articulated before he could ask for guidance.

The old man chuckled. "No, have you ever seen it before?"

"Several times."

He nodded thoughtfully, as if I'd resolved some tedious mathematical formula tangled up in his head. Eventually the plane's rubber wheels hit pavement, and my whole body throttled forward, my stomach doing backflips, and then the man spoke again.

"This, my dear, is my journey's crown jewel, my golden chalice, my lost Ark! Most folks I know visit Pa-lah-low for the Phallic Rock. They want that stroke of childbearing luck. But I say, forget all that bullcrud. I'm here for the aw-paw-paw-nay."

I didn't respond. Probably I was too busy collecting 'ōpala scrunched in my seat pocket, the mess at my feet. Gagging at his spoiled pronunciations. I was waiting for the plane to quit moving already and for my grams to pay attention to the frantic wrinkles of stress wrapping over my face, turning me into an old, worried wāhine. Never before had I flown on a plane without my mother to hold my hand. But Grams was busy talking story with the flight attendant, with whom she shared Kaunakakai as a hometown, and the only person whose attention I held was this old white man's.

The plane's engine spit forth a side-splitting cry, and then the propellers stopped propelling, and everything went still. The honeymooners, folded into each other like the suctioned legs of octopus, exchanged a wet and sloppy kiss. My grams slapped the māhū attendant with a hiccupy laugh. The man left his hand on my shoulder, his grip a furnace.

"Know what a phallus is, girl?" he asked.

I shook my head, a gesture that elicited his own congested chuckle.

"You will soon enough!"

I wiped away his spittle that'd settled on my forearm. Then my grams ushered me up, up, out of the damn plane.

THREE DAYS WAS the scheduled duration of our trip. Three days on Molokai, just me and my grams and the entirety of an 'ōiwi 'ohana I had yet to meet. We were there under the guise of supporting this 'ohana—Saturday was my cousin Kamea's high school graduation—though my mother saw the trip differently. Every summer since she'd turned ten, Mom had suffered six torturous weeks on Molokai, cleaning houses and peeling sand from between her thighs and watching old uncles get wasted on lukewarm Primo. On her last day, some relative would drive her north through a congestion of ironwoods to touch Kaule o Nānāhoa. Her mother, my grams, hailed from Kaunakakai, which made Molokai our family's homeland. She'd hoped to share both the 'āina and the rock with her grandchildren at least once in her life, just as my mother vowed never to return to that wretched island and rock again.

So, a compromise: I would spend the long weekend with Grams, so long as we steered clear of the family tenements and lodged instead at Hotel Molokai. My brother was deemed too young for such a journey (more significantly, he was a boy), and so enjoyed the luxury of remaining at home with our parents. Who knows what fun he got up to that weekend without me. On my last day there, a Sunday, Grams would drive me to Pālā'au to touch the rock. *The Phallic Rock*, according to the old man on the plane. While my grams busied herself catching up with the hotel's only concierge, who also happened to be a fellow Molokai High School grad, I was chewing on my cuticles and thinking about penises.

Once pau with her jovial high school reunion, Grams led me through the open-air lobby and around the corner, where I observed the dark wood exterior and its steep A-frame scaffolding. Somewhere in the lobby, I read a placard that described the hotel's design as "Polynesian thatched architecture." I squinted. All I really saw were sliding screen doors, dusty jalousies, and too many tiki torches screwed into the dirt. Capping the property was a shingled and flared roof, offering slats of shade that did little to curb the awful midsummer heat. My duffel strap bore down on my shoulder; my muscles ached terribly. I sweated. From the back of the property, I watched waves pitch and simmer at Kamiloloa Beach. Haole tourists slouched in Tommy Bahama beach chairs, boiling like poached eggs. No locals as far as I could see.

"Help Grams with this, will you, honey?" A strip of metal dug into my side. It was a key, held stiff in my grams's frail, manicured hand.

I opened the door with a great struggle while Grams ferried her giant rolling suitcase into the room. Too giant for a brief weekend getaway. We stepped into what felt like the dark cave of a shark's mouth. A gust of hot wind slapped at my body. The floors were archaic and creaked below us, while the stained walls and precarious exposed beams depressed me. Grams retired her pink nail file to a plywood folding table then breathed a sigh of what I could only imagine was pleasure. Finally, she was home.

I was not. I explored the sad room, the floors weathered in loose spirals of sand, bumping into furniture, feeling bereaved. Grime was everywhere, threatening allergies and other dismal futures. I climbed the rickety wooden ladder screwed into the floorboards and emerged in a squat loft furnished by a twin mattress, two pillows, and nothing else. This was to be my bedroom. Downstairs, rectangular windows were laden with dust, their corners glued permanently shut.

Sweat collected in a crown around my forehead, under my growing breasts. What I would give in exchange for a cool blast of air-conditioning! (Back home, my parents had opened a separate savings account a few years back, where they reserved funds for a state-of-the-art central air system. After four years, their scrupulousness was rewarded with an enormous cooling contraption, later installed by a charming hapa man from HVAC Hawaii who glanced a bit too long at my asymmetrical breasts, then offered me a melted peppermint candy fished from his workpants.) But alas, there was no utility in sight, just a quaint, humid room pulsing with warmth and a rattan ceiling fan with blades carved to resemble monstera leaves pushing a weak breeze through the space.

"So maika'i, huh, honey?" Grams asked.

"Yes, definitely."

But there was no time for us to dwell in the maika'i. The 'ohana were on their way—my grams's sister, Judy, and her husband, Wally, and their youngest son Kalahiki, whom I'd never met but who was apparently three years older than me—and we had so much to do, so many places to sightsee and to explore. Tomorrow we had their oldest Kamea to cheer on as he received his high school diploma. Was I excited? Not in the least. What I'd hoped to do in that moment, more than anything else, was to call my mother. I wanted my body lulled and calmed by the tender wisps of her voice. But there was no telephone in the hotel room, and when I asked after one, Grams laughed and laughed.

"Oh, honeygirl, this Kaunakakai."

RECENTLY I HAD made a curious discovery about my body, and that was this: when I sat a particular way on a stool, a bench, a chair, really anything with hard, pronounced edges, I could move around enough to feel a current of pleasure jolt through me like electricity. I didn't think on it sufficiently to isolate where in my lower torso this stimulation occurred, but I did make a habit of it, so long as no adults were present to catch me in the act. I didn't know with certainty if what I was doing was wrong, though my gut feeling convinced me this discovery was meant for me and me alone. No girl could be afforded such a pleasure without the accompanying shame with which to share it. Isn't that why it's called a guilty pleasure?

In any case, I met my cousin Kalahiki at a simple local diner, where we sat along the cook counter and feasted on grilled mahimahi and gravy burgers and shumai saimin despite the whipping 90-degree heat. We sat on swiveling green bar stools—all flat cushioning and rounded corners. I drank tepid water, no ice, from a light-brown tumbler. My great-aunt, Judy, was arrestingly handsome; gamine in build, with a sharp, vulpine face, she wore a proud kānaka tan and was difficult to look at in one sweep. I couldn't understand it. No one in our family looked like her. We were wāhine of round build, and we married into our likeness. Yet somehow my grams's baby sister, nearly twenty years her junior, appeared from a different lineage entirely. Her husband looked like her, but darker and even skinnier, as if someone had stretched him out with a baker's rolling pin. No muscle here; rather, he was rangy like a beanstalk, dimensioned only by a gut of fat around his middle. They dressed in drabby clothes, their armpits ringed in sweat. There was a fierceness to their expressions that made them terrible to look at, so instead I looked at Kalahiki.

Who was nothing like his parents, really. In fact, Kalahiki could be said to be the ugliest and fattest boy I'd met in my brief thirteen years. Aside from his disproportionate figure (he'd inherited our family's obesity and his father's broomstick height), Kalahiki suffered from acute eczema, a terrible skin condition that turned his arms, legs, and neck a tapestry of roseola patches. His left earlobe, distended like the lobes of the late Gautama Buddha, was punctured by a mammoth fake diamond. And then there were his teeth—terrible! Malformed and ragged and stained yellow like the hushed glow of streetlamps, his teeth bowed in a way that made it impossible to look anywhere but his mouth. So grotesque were his teeth and his body, and still he grinned supremely, chatted vociferously, asked so many questions about me and answered every question I posed in generous detail.

He spoke so fast and furiously, his mother slapped him on the side of his head.

He winced. He slowed down.

After lunch, I hoped we'd do a bit of walking, stretch our legs after all that sitting in the thick indoor heat. But Wally had bad knees, and Judy was plain lazy. Grams then paced alarmingly slowly in front of us, sidewalk scalding the bottoms of our slippers, and Kalahiki hung back with me, smacking on some gum while I told him about the city back home.

"My house, it's super close to downtown. I can walk to pretty much any restaurant. There are lots of sparkly towers that go glassy at night. Also lots of traffic."

I glanced around the wide streets, not a single traffic light in sight.

"Sounds like one place right out of the movies."

His grin was astonishing. It would not leave his face.

"I mean, this place is cool, too." I stumbled through these words, but Kalahiki only laughed through his protuberance of front teeth.

"No need lie, ah? Get one backwards world over here. One day I going get out. Maybe I come Honolulu, visit you?"

A glimmer exploded from his dark face. I pressed my thighs together as if an unpleasant odor might leak out.

We parted ways near Kiowea Beach Park, the spot where Judy informed us Kamea's graduation party would take place tomorrow night, following the ceremony. They crammed into a battered gray pickup, Kalahiki waving from behind the window, then split. Grams and I had a car, too, a tiny Nissan rental, though possibly she was a reader of minds and asked if I'd like to take a walk, maybe stop for some shave ice just up the street. At the heavy diner lunch, my stomach had tightened into an obstinate fist, and I hadn't eaten much. I was convinced I missed my mother too terribly to eat anything. Then again, what was shave ice if not a beverage rendered solid? And I had to drink; otherwise, I'd dehydrate and die.

We walked slowly past a series of churches: Church of the Nazarene, Ierusalema Pōmaikaʻi, Kūlana, Kalaiakamanu Hou. We stopped at a wide, grassy lot where there stood a precarious wooden construction, tented poorly to provide simple slats of shade. Deconstructed pallets buttressed the shave ice counter, where I asked a friendly uncle named Mike for a small strawberry with li hing powder and condensed milk. Grams ordered a large banana, also topped with li hing and condensed milk, and vanilla ice cream.

"You went give me too much, aunty!" he exclaimed, holding Grams's ten-dollar bill in his fist.

"Not even, no ʻack! Keep ʻum, okay? And say hi to Sherri for me."

"She going be so bummed she missed you! Mahalo nui, aunty!"

Mike handed us our shave ice in white paper cones, each one enormous. I licked a dribble of strawberry syrup that'd spilled down my hand. We sat in soft-strap chairs and watched the waves roll in off Kiowea beach.

"I used to come here every weekend when I was your age," Grams said wistfully. She consumed her shave ice like my mother: first sipping the pond of syrup collecting in the cup's vertex, then digging her wooden spoon into the icy mound. "When I had your mama, Papa and I would bring her back every summer and treat her to the biggest shave ice she liked after we stopped at Pālā'au."

"The Phallic Rock," I said, licking cool flakes from my bottom lip. Despite the pitched tent, my shave ice had already half melted into a blood-red pond.

My grams looked down at me, shocked, like I'd just revealed the truth of how charming I found Kalahiki.

"Your mama went tell you that?"

"The . . . the guy on the plane. The bird-watcher guy. He was showing me his book . . ."

Grams rolled her eyes, clicking her tongue while my words trailed off and away, into the roaring sea.

"Haole," she muttered under her breath. "Listen, honeygirl, we don't call 'um that, okay? We speak the 'ōlelo Hawai'i name, Kaule o Nānāhoa. Your mama went tell you the story?"

I shook my head. My mother had. Still, I hoped to hear the tale again, as kneaded in my grams's mind.

"It went start way, way back, before the haoles came and took over our land. We had one god, Nānāhoa, who went help kāne make babies with their wāhine. He went live up in Pālā'au, happily with his wife, Kawahuna. One day, Huna went catch the bugga making eyes at one young girl. Haumia! So 'āniha, this guy, he went slap his wife and give her lickins so that she went fall down the cliff and turn to stone. When he went ma-ke, Nānāhoa went turn stone, too, beside his wife. Now he stay Kaule o Nānāhoa, the rock we going visit on Sunday. Kānaka believe his stone get strong fertility powers. People who no can have babies come from all over the islands for touch the stone. His spirit helps them come fertile again."

"I like that story," I said.

Grams let loose a big-throated laugh. "Oh, honeygirl, that's the best part! It's not just one story—it stay real! Know how I know?"

A flicker of pleasure in her eye, then, and then I did.

"You touched the stone, too?"

"Of course!" she slapped her knee, sending a spray of banana syrup through the overgrown fountain grass. "And not just me, but my mama, too. And her mama, and her mama before that. Your mama went touch the stone when she was your age—cuz of this, she was able for have you and Kainoa. Now you going follow in our footsteps so that one day, you can be a mama, too."

I fidgeted in my seat, probing the cheap plastic for any solid purchase that would send those shivers down my thighs, deep into my gut. It was a residual desire left over from lunch, when Kalahiki flashed his terrible teeth and I knew I was in trouble.

"You like be a mama someday, honeygirl?" Grams asked me.

But I was too busy shifting in my seat, working to flick synapses of pleasure from between my legs, to consider her question and all it might carry.

HOTEL MOLOKAI HAD a roach infestation, though apparently this was news to only me. That night, I tried my best to find rest in the loft, but what with Grams's incorrigible snoring and the black flicker of roaches, each one the size of a baby's fist, scuttling across the exposed rafters, thready antennae flitting forward as if in a dance, sleep eluded me. In the middle of the night, I hauled my one pillow from the loft, descended those precarious stairs, and settled for the evening in the romantic sway of the beachside hammock.

Suspended a foot above the dewy grass, I rocked in the hammock with the swing of a tiny pendulum. No chance did I have at finding a hardness here to explore this new development of my body, so instead I pondered

Grams's question for a while, until my brain coiled into tight braids and the very word *mama* put me to sleep.

I tried to call my mama when I woke up. Despite the pitiful service in Kaunakakai, I knew the front desk had at least one phone: a tightly wound black cord dangling from the desk like the corkscrewed tail of a pig. With Grams busied in the shower, I scurried away from flighty roaches and considered my options. Would she buy my claim that there was an emergency only my mother could address? Would the auntie working the front desk? It was unlikely. Equally unlikely was endearing Grams to my plight by exposing my truth: that I missed my mama, that all I needed was a single stone of her voice to assure me she was fine, everything would be fine, I would be okay. Plus, I cringed at the thought of making this request to anyone, let alone my nearest relative. Even at thirteen, I knew I'd gone far too many years to utter the appeal *I need my mother.*

Instead of talking to Grams, then, I microwaved a mug of tap water, then downed it in several gulps to feel my throat scorched in pain. I burned my tongue and bottom lip, so there. My distraction for the day. I took a rubber slipper to the enormous exoskeleton of a B52, then left the pale guts splayed out on the kitchen tile as a warning to its friends. When my grams emerged from the bathroom, steam frazzling her hair and her sallow skin dewy with age, I did not disclose how I missed my mother. I don't think I said anything at all.

The day unfurling before us was to be chaotic and eventful. I'd never attended a high school graduation before, but I imagined a jovial affair thronged with bodies, licks of sweat brushing up against us while we hurried to lei and honi the recent grads. On our way to the ceremony, Grams and I stopped at a roadside lei stand, purchased newly threaded lei of pīkake and ginger, poniʻmōʻī for Judy as a gesture of good faith to the mother. (I hadn't spent enough time with her to garner a fair-enough read, though after she again throttled Kalahiki on the back of his neck at the diner, I felt confident in my instinct to keep my distance.) After driving for miles through disrobed fields and simple emerald plains, the scent of florals sopping up what little air our rental car contained, Grams pulled into a sun-drenched gravel lot behind an unassuming brick building dressed in balloons and with sad green ribbons taped to its rafters. A banner reading CONGRATS GRADS shivered in the breeze. We walked through a covered hall then emerged in an open corridor, where a paltry crowd of twenty or so people had gathered for the festivities. Their board shorts and ragged shirts displeased me. That morning, I had taken great care in selecting my outfit, peeling the tangles from my hair and wiping my eyes' collected gunk. I couldn't believe these people. Did they bear no consideration for the way they presented themselves? Or was I, yet again, the child overthinking things?

The graduation carried forth with little fanfare. Standing on a stage furnished from stacks of plywood were four impending grads, one of whom was Kamea. While I'd only just met Kalahiki, I'd met his brother Kamea several times prior. Though technically Grams's nephew, Kamea treated her with the affection and respect of a son, and so our family understood him to be her favorite. She'd hosted him every summer since I was a baby, though I remembered him only in flashes: a game of Uno he'd let me win, the white-bellied kajiki he taught me to descale, a tunnel we carved into the sand. The Kamea standing onstage now was exceedingly tall, filled out, confident. He had bad acne like me, and the outdoor ceremony seemed to pull the sweat from his very pores. Like his four fellow graduates, a formless blue gown draped his frame in a frumpy way that reminded me of my mattress on the floor of the Hotel Molokai loft.

The graduation, like all of Molokai I'd witnessed so far, disappointed me. Or perhaps I was simply in a perpetually poor mood from too much time away from my mother.

My spirits lifted, however, almost immediately at the close of the ceremony when Kalahiki emerged from behind a pockmarked pillar wearing his dopey, toothy grin. I enjoyed considering his mouth in terms of its deficiencies. Those hooked and gnarled teeth—they endeared me to him in a way I couldn't quite understand. Likewise, something formless stirred just below my waistline in a way that encouraged me to seek out the nearest chair or stool—hell, even a toilet seat would do, so long as I kept my underwear on. The gleeful chatter that enveloped the corridor once the students received their diplomas was nothing but a blanket distraction to the ringing of bells between my legs.

Bells rang out through the corridor, too. Then we migrated to Kiowea Park, where it seemed at least two other grads and their truckfuls of 'ohana had gathered to pā'ina. Sea-swept uncles busted out their hibachi grills, their fuzzy speaker systems and Styrofoam coolers filled with Hawaiian ice and Heineken—the local drink of choice. I met several distant family members whose names sprinted past me, along with their bodies. They relaxed themselves into the crutch of beach chairs, against benches flaking with peeling paint. They let their fat leak out of their shorts. After a few drinks, Grams appeared lighter and pliable. She popped the tab off a Primo can, spraying me with foam, insisting I take a sip.

I tried the beer to the sound of pitching waves and the Brothers Cazimero crooning *aloha* through the hāla trees. Grams and the 'ohana cheered this milestone, then let their attention wander elsewhere. Left unsupervised, left motherless and sad, I drank the beer to its bitter end. Near the sandy shoreline, a cluster of guests plucked slack-key melodies and strummed gorgeous koa ukulele. Guests helped themselves to the enormous aluminum trays of kālua pig and squid lū'au, lau lau steamed and sodden, watery beef stew boiled with wedges of potato and carrot. I watched a bowl of raw 'opihi picked off in minutes. My stomach roared under the weight of my clothes, but my hunger strike persisted. I missed my mother.

That is, until Kalahiki showed up. He brought a red cup of undistinguishable liquid and all his bad teeth to the picnic table where I sat. He sat so close our fleshy bare thighs touched. The heat of Kaunakakai pushed through my flimsy purple dress and dappled my forehead in sweat. He asked me why I wasn't eating.

"Not one for local kine food?"

"I'm just not hungry," I said.

"You never went eat much at Kimo's yesterday, either. Trying for lose weight or what?"

I'd meant to respond with some clever retort, but I was only a teenager, and my thoughts were thick with drink.

"Not trying for say you need lose weight, you know. You one skinny nani wāhine."

"Thank you."

"I no need either, right?" And just like that, Hiki was lifting the hem of his hibiscus-printed button-down, revealing a dimpled belt of pink fat roped around his belly, jiggling the excess flab with one fleshy hand. I winced, my stomach folding into itself like origami.

I stuttered, I smarted. Then, I smiled. He laughed jollily at my discomfort.

A second slap, then, this time walloping his left cheek with a clap so loud I felt it reverberate through my teeth. Judy's severe face swam with a sort of non-presence, as though the dozens of Heinekens she'd consumed had washed away any semblance of propriety. I blinked hard, and when I opened my eyes, Kalahiki's own blinked back tears.

"Ho, just jokes, just jokes!" he cried.

"Why you always gotta try shame us li'dat?" Judy snapped.

And just like that, as quickly and frigidly as she'd appeared, Judy was gone.

I brought him ice. Plunged my hand in a Styrofoam cooler to retrieve four cubes, then bandaged them in sheets of paper towels. When I returned with aid, Kalahiki no longer appeared distressed. His entire face had flushed a deep red, and if I could press a palm to his ear, I imagined a gust of steam would blow into my hand, for he was livid.

"I'm sorry she treats you like that," I said slowly. Barely a teenager and still I knew enough about boys and the skeletal fragility of their pride.

"Is she always like that?" I tried again.

In lieu of a response, Kalahiki brought his hand down on my hot, sticky thigh. He thanked me for the ice. Beyond our tent of suffering, old people danced and sang and genuflected at the hips like they were at a middle school dance. Kamea wore efflorescent wreaths of lei around his neck, whose texture reminded me of a brioche loaf. He looked startlingly handsome. A warm notch of wind nicked the outdoor courtyard. Poor Kalahiki. I wanted to come to his rescue, or at least provide some pragmatic assistance, but couldn't imagine any way to do so. I watched my grams wrap her feeble arms around her sister's waist. Little sparks of glee radiating from her face like firecrackers. My stomach twisted into a new kind of knot, something labyrinthine and permanent.

Was this the motherhood so many of them sought? The slap and recoil and this hot, blossoming pain—was I meant to want this, too?

I asked Kalahiki if he happened to have a cell phone.

"Service here sucks fat boto," he said, sniffling.

SUNDAY, AT LONG last! The roaches descended once again over the floorboards of Hotel Molokai, and so I found myself jostling and turning in the sock of the hammock, the harsh spray of seawater soundtracking my morning arousal. Both hands were in my underwear, submerged down there. Not in a sexual way; just that often at that age, I woke up with a hand or two inside me. When I realized, however, I'd left the privacy of hotel bedsheets for the outdoors, I removed my hands.

Morning was just breaking over the shoreline, sending a liquid sheet of light to tango over the sand and the blue seas. Slats of gold descended through the tree boughs, and the frantic chatter of pigeons filled my head to bursting. I sat up thinking of the revolting old man sitting behind me on the plane. The paperback he displayed proudly, and the way he turned in his mouth 'ōlelo Hawai'i until it was something else entirely. Something as nasty and pilau as him.

HOTEL MOLOKAI

Carefully I swung my legs over the hammock, then worked to regain my balance before finding purchase on solid ground. My gaze shifted mauka, where supposedly Mount Kamakou met Maunaloa in a beautiful pocket of valleys and cliffs. (Though I couldn't identify it then, Kalaupapa was also in sight.) I wondered where, among this tapestry of buffs, greens, and golds, I might find Nānāhoa's dead body stilled to stone. What distance separated me from this magical rock that might aid one day in making me a mother? There was so much I still didn't know.

I'd heard my mother joke about the rock, well before this trip even took shape in our minds. She didn't use the old man's term *phallic*; instead, she flat-out dubbed it the Penis Rock while rubbing her own crotch and giggling. My father, ever the proper Protestant, clicked his tongue at her then left the room. She took a cigarette to her lips then cindered a corner of paper napkin to ash. She glanced at me, dipping a wedge of mango in shoyu; at my brother, colliding his toy trucks in a blast of sound. She shook her head.

"A rock did not get me pregnant," she declared.

I loved my mother immensely. But I also believed in the rock's innate power to gift me a child when I was of an appropriate age. I couldn't understand her resistance to it. I'd heard tales from various members of the 'ohana about how difficult it was for our wāhine to get pregnant. I even remember peeling through the pages of my fragile-spined dictionary to make sense of the word *barren*. What was so wrong with not having keiki? I'd think of Miss Tanigawa, the single woman who lived in a quaint hutch of a cottage just across the street from us. She was blissfully old, unmarried and without children, and every time I saw her, she was stooped low over her vegetable garden, inspecting some root or soil and grinning like a madwoman. Incredible! Not even my grams, whom I'd known as jovial by nature, grinned with such unbridled euphoria.

Was this the happiness reserved for adults out of their youth? Or for women who lived delightedly alone?

Grams was awake when I returned to the room. She didn't grill me on my whereabouts or demand to know why I hadn't left a note. Instead, she sat around the plywood table, smiling, tending to her nails.

"You excited, honeygirl?" she asked, fiddling with the tip of her nail file. "Once in a lifetime, this day! I'm just so proud for share it with you."

She blew on the hood of her left thumbnail, sending a tiny cloud of dust in a rise and fall to the floorboards. Sand I'd tracked inside now webbed between my toes, stuck to my soles like wads of gum. I swallowed what felt like an enormous coral head, then asked Grams very quietly if there was any chance I could borrow a phone, either from her or the front-desk lady. Her grin fell away then. She stared at me, perturbed.

"How come you need one phone?"

Because I miss my mother terribly. Because I can't touch this stupid Penis Rock without hearing her tell me everything will be okay. Please.

"It's no big deal," I said. "I wanted to talk to Mom, but—"

"Your mama's busy, sweets. She takes such good care of you. Try give her this break!"

I didn't know what to say. I nodded, and then Grams was heaving herself from that sinking lounge chair with a cry—*oisha!*—and instructing me to my duffel, where she would help me pick out what to wear.

"Special occasion, you know. Like yesterday's pāʻina, except sacred. Gotta be on your best behavior, too, though I not worried about that one bit. So maikaʻi, you."

She ruffled my hair like I imagined one might pet a dog, a very good boy.

Later, I fixed my hair in the bathroom mirror. I stared at the sad girl blinking back at me for a very long time.

After several minutes of back-and-forth deliberation, we settled on an outfit to accommodate both of our tastes: scoop-neck ivory blouse, clunky jeans skort shorn just above my knees. Rubber slippers—they were the only footwear I'd packed—but I was meant to wear my twizzled hair up and out of my face, including those fraying baby flyaways. At first I got dressed quickly, deliberately, beside my grams's ungiving mattress, but then a knock at the door sent me fleeing, barricading me and the adolescent shame of my body in the bathroom, from where I could discern awful Aunt Judy's wide, hairy laugh and the stomping footfalls of Uncle Wally behind her. I took my time then, paying attention to the hard clasp of the skort's hem into my innocent flab when I buttoned it. I was horrified by the thought of my own belly's inflation, feared that one day I might face the same dismal protuberance of limbs and lungs that my relatives did. Or maybe, like my shockingly slender aunt, I'd be spared through hard exercise and a meticulous, likely exhausting attention to the food I let pass through my mouth. I tugged the rounded neck of the blouse over my head, took note of the folds that'd settled under the fabric like soft ripples in the sea. I frowned. Why did this seem such a woman's worry?

Outside, the hotel room had assumed a new air of grease and heat. Judy was reclining slack in Grams's bed, bare thighs splayed out like butchered flanks, while Uncle Wally sat in the only other lounge chair—*my* chair, peeling back the corners of lufting parchment paper from some mysterious baked good.

Kalahiki did not come with them.

I joined the 'ohana around the table. When I leaned toward the package, I brushed up too close to Wally, who smelled mealy and in need of a shower. I sprang back. He took his time with the package, long enough to irk Judy.

"Try work faster, ah? I stay so hungry!"

"You like for do 'um?"

She growled like a yappy Chihuahua that believes itself immense. He growled like the German shepherd behind our house, tethered to a post by a thick chain and seething.

Grams clicked her tongue at them both. "How come you gotta act li'dat?"

Judy's shoulders slumped. She wore her silvered hair like a frazzled coif on her head, and her whole face was punchy with red and sweating. "Still got plenny for clean at Kiowea. I tried for get Hiki for help, but went his room this morning, and bugga stay *gone*."

"Selfish boto," Wally mumbled.

"Wherefore he went?"

"Probably for ho'oipoipo with that nasty girl in Ho'olehua. Tries for tell us she stay his ipo, ha! Like anyone'd want his fat ass."

"Get one girlfriend?" Grams asked.

But Wally just snorted in response.

"He wishes."

I brought my arms to my chest, an unkind breeze bearing through the open door. I needed to sit down, but all the seats were taken. I could join the crawl of roaches, red ants, insects of every ilk making a home of our hotel room floor. Did Kalahiki really have a girlfriend? Was he in love with this girl from Ho'olehua, or were they together as a matter of convenience? And why on earth did I care? Even at thirteen, I was cognizant of rules prohibiting cousins from finding happiness together. Allowing this knowledge to seep into my chest and heart, however, was another story entirely.

My head was brimming with questions, enough for someone to take a ladle to it and scoop them into a bowl. But the grown-ups were busy—making plans, talking shit, discussing other grown-up matters. I waited patiently in the bathroom doorway, feeling skin-scraped and raw, while Uncle Wally unwrapped and brought his hands to a giant loaf of Kanemitsu Bakery sweet bread, ripping it into bruised, asymmetrical parts. The bread smelled yeasty and baked in butter, coils of steam pushing off its surface. My stomach rumbled furiously, but I turned away all the same.

IN THE RENTAL car, Grams proudly declared she had a plan and the plan was this: Today, we would make the drive to Pālā'au so she could introduce me to Kaule o Nānāhoa. Before all that, however, we would stop at Kiowea to help Judy and Wally with cleanup of the pā'ina. Probably there would be leftovers, however stale and fly-tainted, so we could eat there before hitting the road once again for Pālā'au.

I squirmed around in the front seat but not in search of some interior rapture; just that I was thinking a lot about the Penis Rock, and it made me uncomfortable.

Grams noticed. "What, get ants in your pants or what?"

I chilled out after that.

We pulled onto the weedy field of Kiowea Park, where suggestions of last night's party littered picnic benches, inlets, patches of grass. Two hibachi grills still exhaled smoke from their clunky grates. Everywhere there were scattered corpses of Heineken bottles, more bottles than I'd seen lining supermarket shelves. I watched Uncle Wally, fat black trash bag in hand, stooped over this glass cemetery, collecting the empties. Each one tumbled into the bag with a giant clang. I drilled my eyes shut through an especially sharp clatter, and when I opened them, Kalahiki was here.

Judy was yelling. I heard little from my hillside perch under a bluff of kiawes, their skeletal boughs rasping in the wind. So much wind abraded the hair from my face that I struggled to hear much of anything beyond the shaking leaves above me, so when Judy pounced on Kalahiki, moving quicker and more exacting than I'd seen any of this 'ohana move prior, I saw the damage she inflicted well before I heard its repercussions. When his cries made their way to me, I dropped my own trash bag and ran.

HOURS LATER, AND I did not run to the Penis Rock. I let my feet fall heavy and flat into the dust; I dragged them like heiau stones to the sacrifice. I was so distracted thinking of what we'd all let happen to Kalahiki back at Kiowea that I didn't see the spindling root system clawing from the dirt, didn't know this 'āina could hurt me so. I fell. I landed on my knees and palms, and then there was blood, enough to warrant a detour through the Pālā'au State Park women's restroom for an intense cleaning of the cuts. My inherent clumsiness would not send us packing. We'd flown all this way, after all, to be here.

Standing there, blood clotting where I'd skinned the surface of my limbs, I didn't feel like a woman, like someone meant to someday be a mother. I didn't feel like much of anything, really, except a terribly young girl who'd afforded violence and missed her own mother dearly. I'd see her again tomorrow, of course, so long as our Cessna didn't jostle a propeller or snag a wheel, sending us all plummeting into the Pacific.

How grateful I should be to have traveled with my grams, who, thanks to her scrupulous attention to the health and beauty of her fingernails, carried with her at all times a toiletry bag of polish and gloss and a nail file and clippers and tweezers and . . . aha! Bandages. She draped a few flesh-colored ones on my wounds and then patted my back with pleasure.

"Can you believe we're here?" she asked, soaking it all in, and I truly could not.

I carried this disbelief around with me like I carried my injuries through the back of Pālā'au's throat. Just

Grams and me, we followed a well-worn trail through sweeping arcs of ironwoods, whose needles papered the path in light brown. No upturned roots, stray boulders that might impede our venture forward. Just a sheared path to travel quickly, quickly, lest the rock lose its magical powers while awaiting our arrival.

I got mean, sometimes, when I was in pain.

Grams seemed fine. The morning's events at Kiowea may have very well existed only in my mind, for Grams wore the look of a wāhine unfazed, moving forward with purpose. I wanted to ask her about the day she first touched Kaule o Nānāhoa—were her fingers splayed out and forced onto the stone by her mother, her grandmother? Or did she gallop to the rock wearing the same emphatic grin she was wearing now? And why couldn't we just become mothers the old-fashioned way? Something about the inheritance of touching the rock didn't sit well with me, though maybe my discomfort had more to do with watching Judy's volatile fists than it did with some prophetic family stone.

After walking the trail for what felt like a few centuries, we emerged at an enormous clearing of felled kukui and more ironwoods, the needles blanketing the 'āina in soft folds of beige. I picked one up just to feel it in my hands. While it appeared razor sharp and frightening, the segmented needle barely bristled my skin. It was soft as a feather. I brought it between my teeth and chewed on it for a while then dropped it on the ground.

The rock gleamed overhead. It did not look like a penis.

I'd seen a penis once only, in fifth-grade math. We were paired two to a desk for an activity involving tiny red blocks and fractions. We did not have a say in our partners. I worked quietly beside Mitch Kam, a rotten-mean athlete who suffered from halitosis and made me suffer even more the closer he got to my face. Mitch tired of the worksheet quickly, and before I could stop him, he rearranged all my blocks to form what looked to me like a long stick nestled firmly between two rocks. I didn't ask him about it.

"Know what this is?" he asked.

I shook my head, not looking at him.

He pinched me, then, curled his fingers around a heft of lower belly flab in a way that wrung the air from my lungs.

"Ouch, quit it."

I glanced down to remove his fingers, and when I did, something floppy and alive had sprung from his pants, like magic. Yes, yes, I understood now that it was a penis. At the time, though, can you imagine my surprise at encountering what looked to me like a dead fish reeled onto dry land, its flesh tender and lined, its scales the color of my own warm insides? The tip of it, too—a dimpled tube like a cap for the tissue—it terrified me. I watched in a strange paralysis as he plucked from the base of the penis a looping black hair no longer than my thumb, analyzed its dimensions, then threw the hair on my lap with a big-bellied chuckle.

The truth is I left his pubic hair on my lap for the remainder of class, and when the bell rang, I pocketed then brought it home and hid it in the bottom drawer of my dresser, the underwear drawer. I never looked for it again, but I knew it was there, and that knowledge cracked open for me the reality of boys and girls, and that knowledge was enough.

This rock did not look like Mitch Kam's fifth-grade penis. Only a few feet tall and pinched near the middle with a wide tip nearly split in two by an enormous fracture, the rock appeared to me more like the breaching head of a honu at sea than it did some magical phallic god cast in stone. It was disappointing. As we approached, we saw there was one other group present, two middle-aged haole couples with hysterical sunburns and matching white sneakers. The taller woman was holding a Dasani water bottle in one hand, a digital camera in the other. She trained the lens on her husband, who had energetically mounted the rock, riding its dimpled ridge like a paniolo straddles the back of a horse. He was grotesquely fat, this man, and middle age had sprayed back his wispy white hair like the parting of the seas, leaving a wide strip of ruddy pink scalp exposed to the elements. He knocked back his head and laughed. The other couple laughed. The tall woman laughed, too, and her arm flab jiggled as she snapped several photos.

I could see from the burn in her cheeks Grams found them revolting. I also knew she would refrain from making a scene as a show of respect—not for them, but for the sacred ʻāina on which we stood. These haoles weren't worth her breath, and so they weren't worth mine.

The man descended the rock clumsily, and Grams turned away while the wife and man exchanged control of the camera. He behind the lens, and the tall woman nestled between the other couple and bearing a reef of crooked teeth and at the count of three and in unison they declared, "Cheese!" *Bad luck*, I thought, and Grams, glimpsing them, grinning.

Some time passed, and eventually the couples hobbled away, leaving me and Grams alone with Kaule o Nānāhoa. I observed her face. She appeared somber, but proud. Her nails were manicured like my mother's, the edges congruous and clean. I let her take my hand and guide me toward the statue in what felt like a hallmark of ritual. Perhaps my ovaries were being fashioned right then and there for future procreation. But what even were ovaries? And what did they look like? Grams clutched my hand so hard I imagined the flesh of my palm flattened to a pulp. She spoke of my mother while we made our way to the stone.

"She was scared, too, you know? It's scary, being so close to all that mana. You not going find nothing like this on Oʻahu. This pure mana from the ʻāina. Molokai mana! But I went held her hand, the whole time. I watched the mana enter her. Then it went happen, and she wasn't scared no more."

I wasn't scared, I thought to myself, each step tugging me closer to my untimely fate. I wasn't scared, but I didn't want to be a mother, either. Not yet, maybe not ever. It shocked me to think our 'ohana's inability to make more children could ever be considered a problem in need of a solution. We didn't care for the children we already had—Judy and Wally had made that clear. Why welcome more keiki into our mess?

I should have asked her. I did not ask her. We brought our barren bodies to the calcified Nānāhoa and asked for something more.

Years later, bent over in the twisting torment of first labor, I would remember the sensation of my hand on that stone with alarming clarity. I would remember its cool, smooth skin and the quick jolt of mana that surged through me, limb to limb to limb. What's more, I would remember the violence inflicted on a son by a mother—Judy's fists beating into Kalahiki's doughy, maturing parts—and the sounds he made. The sounds he could neither swallow nor contain. I remembered how I ran, though I didn't run fast enough, and by the time I reached the flats of Kiowea, the damage had already breached his face, showing deep scratches and lacerations where her wedding ring had lanced his skin; and above all, I remembered how I didn't stop the assault, how I teetered for a moment between action and inaction before rocking back on my heels and leaning into Grams's warning palm on my belly—*not our place*—though I was certain it was our place, and so was she, for her own hand was trembling—where else were we meant to be?—and how even after Wally strolled over to disengage his wife, even after she removed her hands, Kalahiki wouldn't look at me, and later, while he walked slowly toward his bike, he wouldn't answer my series of questions—*are you okay? does that always happen? do they hurt you all the time? why don't you fight back? why didn't you do anything to stop it?*—no, he just got on his bike and pedaled away and left, and he didn't even wave or shaka because there was nothing there left for him that mattered, nothing and no one who cared enough to stop his pain. I remembered it all, with each contraction, each excruciating push, and I squeezed my husband's hand, watched my thighs quake in a forever misery, and I swore then and every day since I would never lean into passivity ever again, no—I would scrape and strike, smash and claw and cry and cuff anyone who came close to touching my baby, my child.

I would never return to Molokai, though I would thank Nānāhoa in every sleep for giving me my child.

Aiko, the Writer

Had spent the last decade drafting a Night Marchers–themed collection, so you can imagine her surprise and her horror when, a day after its completion, the papers on which she'd penned her masterpiece began to vibrate. She'd never seen printer paper vibrate before, much less without provocation. Possibly she was hallucinating, her sleep as of late errant and unresponsive, her attentions everywhere and elsewhere. Wary, she tucked the pages into the Ewa-most drawer of her desk before endeavoring to pack for her upcoming travels, yet another benign task on which to waste her time.

Admittedly, she was bad at doing things that were not writing. Which was why she'd made such a conscientious effort to fill her hours with writerly events, with deadlines, with anything germinative and relevant to the writing craft. With speaking engagements centered on the writing life. The day her draft collection began to vibrate, Aiko was scheduled to board a plane for Austin, Texas, where the literary community of Austinites was waiting to sop up her brilliance at a writers' panel titled "The Art of Place." It would be her first engagement since the sales disaster. She took comfort in the fact that no one in the audience, not her fellow panelists or likely even the conference director, knew of her literary troubles.

After several hours of deliberation, Aiko resolved to bring the manuscript on the flight. Likely she'd imagined the pages' strange undulations, wild and wily was her capacity for creation. And even if the pages vibrated a bit, so what? She could sit on them if she had to. Plane seats were incommodious anyway, always deficient in tailbone support, in the casting of one's coccyx. A chunk of papers might do her perch on an eight-hour flight some good.

Aiko hole-punched then bindered her manuscript, slotting the pages in her carry-on between speaking notes and an advance copy of her colleague's memoir, through which she had yet to make her way. She honi'd farewell to her husband, the physicist, then snaked through the taxing security line at HNL, removed her laptop and her shoes for the screening checkpoint, presented then pocketed her ID and boarding pass, bought a Starbucks coffee, filled her water bottle, charged her phone. Several emails from her agent awaited her attention. By the time boarding began, she had answered none of them, she had forgotten about the manuscript entirely.

The flight was unexceptional—cramped quarters, several downed lorazepam—and when she arrived in Austin later that afternoon, Aiko was positively certain her brain had fabricated all that vibrating nonsense, possibly from her lack of sleep but also as a defense mechanism against touching the collection too soon. Yes, she had her agent to answer to, but more than that was the throbbing hum of her late mentor Lacey's sage warning about approaching a work before it has fully steeped. You mustn't, under any circumstances, broach revisions to your draft until it has adequately collected a scrim of dust in "the drawer." Yet Aiko was pleased. Finally she'd bent to readerly expectations of an Indigenous writer, but the draft was far from finished. Oh, how marvelous her days ahead would be if the manuscript could revise itself! How lovely to imagine she would never again face another shameful book sales failure, the Night Marchers her cultural redeemers. (In the voice of her agent, a white man: *Give the readers what they want!*)

At the baggage claim, though, the vibrations teased through the fake leather of her carry-on, a distressing development that delayed her attention to the revolving belt transporting her checked suitcase. What color was it? What make, what brand? Her bag, it buzzed against her thigh. She felt the footfalls of Night Marchers descending the sloping Pali in her ligaments and her bones. She thought of her tūtū, those warring words, and her warning: *Do not write about anything kapu.*

Do not write about the Night Marchers.

Aiko retrieved her checked bag then trundled through a parking garage, searching for a ride service and cell phone service and a patch of shade under which to shade herself. Already a slick film of sweat lathered her limbs, wetted the crevices her breasts made, and Aiko thought fondly of the trade winds she'd left back home. In an email blast delivered last week to all participants, the conference organizer warned of Austin's ruthless late-summer heat, a caveat Aiko had assumed was intended for those feeble Northeasterners, with their money and their coats. She thought herself a kānaka bastion of heat. Now here she was, waiting for a ride share to usher her through the city, gummy from the sink of Texas humidity and her own briny sweat.

When the ride finally did show, Aiko insisted on loading her own suitcase before occupying the seat behind the driver. She cowered to inspect her manuscript while the man spoke of the "tragedy" that was the city of Austin housing its unhoused in nearby hotels. She worked very hard not to listen to his insults and instead to recite the collection's working title in her head: *A Catalogue of Kānaka Superstitions*. She wanted to feel its syllables between her fingers. She knew it was too long, far too academic to please its future marketers, yet something about the rhythm of its vowels soothed her. Soothed her until she was holding the pages in her hands and the letters started to tremble once again.

Aiko gasped. The driver peered at her through his mirror, asked if she was okay. But Aiko hadn't been okay for a very long time. She donned her best smile and said yes.

Only when she finally got settled in her hotel room did she call her husband. The physicist was terse and distracted over the phone, though fourteen years of marriage had inculcated in her an awareness of his swings in register, his moods erratic, his voice bloated. She could tell he was concerned she hadn't called sooner. Without prompting, she apologized. The physicist said he accepted her apology. They spoke briefly about his day at the lab, briefer still about Aiko's panel discussion scheduled for tomorrow afternoon. The manuscript was retucked into her binder, the binder bunked inside her bag. Her notes were scattered somewhere. So long as she kept her husband on the phone, Aiko had a reasonable excuse not to think about the vibrating pages. So long as they were speaking, she was obliged to honor her responsibility, her marital duty as a wife. How preposterous that she had spent so many years as a wife!

But the physicist hung up too soon, and then Aiko was stretched supine on the palatial king mattress, hair fallen over her forehead, her own words buzzing around her.

BEFORE FINISHING THE draft manuscript, before putting her fingers to the keyboard or scribbling ideas on notecards or even picking up a goddamn pen, before the idea of a Night Marchers–themed collection even took form in her brain, Aiko was visited by her tūtū's spirit, her akua lapa, in her sleep. She knew the visitor to be her tūtū because just as her eyelids started to flutter, Aiko had spotted a green house gecko plodding across the sloped ceiling a few feet from her resting face. She closed her eyes, let sleep take her. The gecko was her family's 'aumakua, her many generations of ancestors manifested as mo'o with their tiny adhesive pads, flattened figures, wide and phantasmagoric eyes. Kapu to kill one, even accidentally. Those eyes, little buttons of black, were the last things she saw before drifting to sleep, and then she saw her tūtū.

Tūtū Gracie was her mother's mother, a boisterous, acerbic woman with many opinions and several outdoor cats. Hailing from Kaunakakai, Molokai, Gracie was cantankerous and oppressive, yet widely loved. When she died of complications from leukemia, nearly two hundred people showed up for her funeral. In the months following her death, it appeared she had assumed the expected mo'o form and could now ascend walls, peel her way through crevices, and communicate with the living. She could communicate with her granddaughter.

I want you to be extremely careful with the words you deliver to the universe, she'd warned Aiko. *I know you are a writer. It's important to be a writer whose work retains a strong, ethical framework.*

AIKO, THE WRITER

In life, Aiko had never heard her tūtū speak so mannered. *Punctilious*, maybe, was the word for it. When talking to Aiko, tūtū only ever used pidgin. The change in speech alarmed her, far more than the woman's transformation into a house gecko.

There are ways to tell Hawaiian stories and ways to make Hawaiian stories vulnerable to the white hand. You'll need to be extremely careful with your choices.

Aiko, drowsy and dozing, asked for clarification.

Don't bother with accessibility. Even when you write white, the white readers won't make sense of it. Bother with specificity. Be exacting and specific. Write in 'ōlelo Hawai'i when you can. Write dialogue in pidgin, because dialect is important. Most importantly, honor the kapu. Do not write about what you cannot write about.

Aiko didn't understand all the way. She nodded.

You understand?

She continued nodding.

You cannot write about the Night Marchers.

Okay, Aiko said.

One day you will very much want to, but you can't. You shouldn't. It will bring you terrible luck.

Aiko agreed.

The next morning, Aiko woke exhilarated. She had an extraordinary idea for her new collection.

To say her last project had failed was a glorious understatement. Despite her agent's many warnings against trying to debut with a story collection, Aiko persisted, headstrong and heedless. Worse still was her adamant refusal to embrace her identity as Indigenous, to write the cultural stories readers expected of her. Instead, she wrote benign stories about conceits of interest to her: trauma and its aftermath, isolation, nuanced identity, the female body. Her stories were set in places she'd once inhabited: Bozeman, Montana; Dublin; New Hampshire. To capitulate to the public's exoticized expectations of an Indigenous writer seemed absurd. Instead, she'd spent her twenties working sundry temp jobs by day and writing speculative fiction after hours, using office printers to make copies of her work. By her thirties, she was married to the physicist and had placed a few stories in notable print and online magazines. By thirty-five, she felt confident in her manuscript and welcomed her agent to shop it around. Conditions of the publishing industry, however, weren't welcoming to an Indigenous voice that didn't center its Indigeneity. Plus, dismal public interest in story collections.

Her agent broke the news of editors' indifference over email, a dreadful way to communicate disappointments.

It had taken all of five years and an overnight visit from her tūtū to dust off her humiliations and start writing again. She would not permit entry to the intrusive thoughts beating the door to her brain, her agent's querulous face, his virulent insistence that a story collection just would not sell to publishers. Her extraordinary talent and an acquiescence to white readers would see to its selling, she was convinced. And the idea, far more marketable than any literary 'ōpala she'd scrawled over the past two decades. Its premise was deceptively simple: each story in the collection would center a singular encounter with Night Marchers, the embodied spirits of long-dead Hawaiian warriors who mercilessly kill any mortals in their path. The stories would progress in density and in nuance—from a half-page flash piece to a sweeping novella—before culminating in a confrontation with the Night Marchers, whose scope spans the entire cast of the collection. The Night Marchers, as is custom, would emerge victorious. The collection would cater to those seeking horror, thrills, with the quality of a literary tradition. The collection might make her famous.

The collection was vibrating in her carry-on, demanding to be freed from its restraints.

As for the writers' panel, Aiko was reasonably prepared. She'd been receiving invitations to speak at writers' conferences and MFA seminars and one-day workshops since her feature in *The Atlantic* went almost-viral two years ago. In the piece, Aiko decried the disastrous Hawai'i education system and demanded justice for keiki o ka 'āina. At its time of publication, Aiko wasn't Aiko the writer but Aiko the teacher, a poorly compensated associate professor on tenure track at the University of Hawai'i at Mānoa. While *The Atlantic* didn't change her financial or collegiate standing, it did run ripples through the publishing industry, spotlighting Aiko as one who might impart wisdom to writers early in their careers, writers more like herself than she was willing to concede.

Though often the schools or affiliates would reimburse her travel expenses, Aiko was on her own with lodging and dining. After scrimping and saving, after subsisting off Subway sandwiches and several meat sticks, after her fourth trip of writerly intentions, Aiko decided to treat herself in Austin. She left her manuscript and her conference notes in the carry-on, she unhooked her bra and felt her breasts deflate with glee. She called for room service. She ordered chicken tenders with country gravy and a side garden salad, a glass of pinot grigio. She programmed the television to the comedy station and binged *South Park* as if she were in her twenties again. The hotel room's central air system pulsed frigid air through the vents and quickly ushered Aiko beneath the bed linens. When the food finally arrived, her chicken was cold and the salad greens wilted, but none of it mattered, because Aiko was weary from traveling and ravenous. She ate everything on the tray in a matter of minutes.

Ordering room service reminded her of her tūtū. Admittedly everything reminded her of her tūtū now that she'd defied her, but this especially so because Gracie had a history of ordering room service whenever she traveled. Not like her tūtū was some high maka maka jetsetter; to Aiko's limited knowledge, she'd managed to make it only as far as Oakland, California. But Gracie enjoyed her fair share of kama'āina staycations, each one outfitted with an elaborate room-service spread she consumed in a bathrobe and with chopsticks. Ahi poke and green salad and macaroni salad and kalbi and shoyu chicken—everything she consumed with chopsticks.

And what were chopsticks if not slender spears, unkindled torches begging for a flame? Now chopsticks, *those* reminded her of Night Marchers. Those deadly apparitions about whom warned her parents and her teachers, her 'ohana and especially her tūtū. They were the most savage, formidable forces a mortal might encounter. As Aiko matured from child to adolescent, adolescent to adult, the eerie reality of the Night Marchers superstition stuck; it stoked her fear like gas on a flame.

Aiko tried her best not to think about her tūtū or that awful superstition for the rest of the evening. This was her first time in Austin; she was in town only for the weekend. It was the farthest she'd been requested to travel, and now she was traveling with an actual, completed manuscript in tow. Being a writer was a trip! She shook her head, she laughed to herself. Pages vibrating. What a phenomenal joke!

So she freed the manuscript at last, and then she stripped for a shower. The water spitting from the showerhead was excruciatingly hot, and no matter how insistent she was with the cold-water knob, the heat persisted. Strange. She shampooed swiftly and toweled off, and then she fled the hotel, manuscript tucked under her armpit, for the dive bar across the street.

Tiki-themed and grotesque. Aiko passed through cascading coils of puka shells suspended from the ceiling and ordered a gin and tonic from the bartender in flannel and wearing a wide-brimmed hat. She placed her binder on the bar top. Twangy 'ukulele tunes threaded through the brightly lit hall, a melody that seemed to delight the large groups around her. All of them haoles, though Aiko expected nothing less. The bartender returned with her drink in a rocks glass. At least the A/C was working. Aiko could forgive most anything so long as the physical weather of a space was calibrated to her preference.

She sipped her gin and tonic then opened the binder. Perhaps it wasn't the worst thing in the world, to approach these pages before they breathed. And maybe the vibrations were exactly that—her words breathing, snatching, stretching, expanding to fit the scaffolding of their stories. It was possible she hadn't entirely lost it, that she still had her wits about her, yet with every sip of her drink, Aiko found herself wishing she'd abandoned the manuscript in the hotel, that she'd brought her notes or that awful memoir in its stead.

Unthinking, she called Pamela. Pamela was also in town for the conference. They shared the same mentor in undergrad, spent months of their burgeoning lives writing bad drafts of stories in the library stacks. The last time they'd spoken—to inform each other of their mentor Lacey's passing—Pamela had a different editor, a different wife, while Aiko was pregnant with a fetus she'd eventually lost.

Pamela claimed she was working on her craft talk for tomorrow.

"What if you came and worked on it here?" Aiko asked.

By the time Pamela arrived, a cluster of undergrads had thronged the venue, leaving little room at the bar top and Aiko in distress. Pamela, in contrast, appeared wholly unfazed. She flagged the bartender with an air of measured authority then squeezed past a handsy couple to settle in the stool beside Aiko. Pamela, an Unangan from the Aleutian Islands, wore her feathery brown hair in a loose bun and white wire-rimmed glasses. She was slender, as Aiko had remembered her, but with more pronounced breasts and turquoise veins templing her hands. The ring finger of her left hand was bare.

"It was such a shame to miss you at Lacey's funeral," Pamela said.

To explain it away, Aiko cited exorbitant plane fares.

"I get it. If it weren't for the divorce money, I probably wouldn't have been able to make it myself. Oh yeah, Louise is gone," she shared, gulping down a salt-rimmed margarita and staring at her hands. "We made it all the way to Easter before she got tired of my shit and ran. Oh well. I say life's more fun without her."

Aiko's own hands held down the manuscript. Through the plastic film of the binder cover she could feel the pages stewing, boiling hot, hotter, hot to the touch like the shower at the hotel. She sprung back. She had no idea what Pamela was talking about but acted as though she did. At forty, calling an old friend from undergrad after ordering your second gin and tonic is at best a puzzling mistake.

"You and D—— still going strong?"

Aiko said yes. "We both work so much, work too much, probably, but we're doing fine."

"And the panel, you feeling ready?"

This was a trickier question to address. Aiko explained how she had spent the years since her breakout publication in *The Atlantic* trying to make sense of the absence of Indigenous representation in contemporary literature and why the piece had garnered so much attention. In her mind, it wasn't saying anything novel. This confusion, coupled with her own sustained bouts with impostor syndrome, had deflated her confidence. Who was she to cast judgments on how "Place" did or did not function in contemporary literature? In the literature of her peers? And once those judgments were cast, how would the audience, composed primarily of ambitious but unpublished white writers, actualize her prescriptive thoughts in their own prose? How could she speak with the weight of advocacy? A slippery slope for anyone, much less a writer of her own dissatisfaction.

"I don't have a great deal of experience with public speaking," she added. "But we could use the money, so I came."

Pamela was convinced they were the only Indigenous women speaking at the conference. Along with Aiko, the topic of "Place" would be addressed by a Texan from Odessa, a white man hailing from Sweden, and a white woman based in California's Marin County. All but Aiko were widely and propitiously published. Aiko understood, intuitively, that she was expected to present the Indigenous Perspective. Pamela agreed it was a good idea to come, if only for the money.

"You read Susan's memoir yet?" she asked.

Aiko shook her head, laughing.

They continued in this fashion for over an hour—quipping, drinking, talking shit, and shitting on the literary world that welcomed them only for their Indigenous Perspectives. In summation, Aiko had consumed three gin and tonics and half of Pamela's margarita. Pamela's drinks, Aiko did not keep count. At around seven, Aiko closed out her tab with the new bartender on shift, and Pamela, peering down at the binder, deliberated aloud whether she'd had one too many, because honey, those pages were *moving*.

AND THE PAGES were moving, and Aiko was frightened. She dreaded returning to the hotel alone, sleeping anywhere near her thrumming prose. Always things were buzzing around her: the A/C, her husband's phone, their home printer, her own chaotic thoughts. The last thing she needed was her manuscript palpitating in public, in private while she wired her thoughts for sleep.

Outside the bar, Aiko and Pamela lingered for a beat. With enough gin dripping through her, Aiko proposed that Pamela join her for a nightcap back at the hotel.

"The minibar has Tito's."

"Tito's! My heart. But I need to call my lover. She's expecting me. So good, really, catching up with you!"

They honi'd goodbye. Pamela skirted westward, and Aiko headed south. This time, she held her binder to her chest and imagined her own heartbeat synching with that of her manuscript. The streets of downtown Austin were wide but dirty, unkempt, the sidewalks leaky with humidity. She dreaded crossing the river into South Congress for inscrutable reasons. A Night Marcher would never meet her here, yet the unhoused man bent beneath the bus stop indeed resembled huaka'i pō, a deceased Hawaiian warrior whose spirit continues to haunt the surface world. A Night Marcher.

Aiko made tiny fists, her gritty, untrimmed nails carving dimples in her palms. She breathed in the steamy southern air. She reminded herself: this was Austin, Texas. She was nowhere near the sacred spaces of ka wā 'ōiwi wale nō, where huaka'i pō dwelled. This was the place where she could feel, absurdly, safe.

Because if she were being honest, she hadn't felt safe in Hawai'i for a long time. The island was like a twisted and perverted organ whose guts had spoiled long ago.

Today, haoles outnumbered kānaka ʻōiwi one hundred to one. She knew few folks who still practiced the old traditions, idolized akua, revered and heeded the superstitions of generations past. What's worse, they were all better for it. Her relatives who'd conformed to the ways of the white residents had made themselves rich. Impossibly, they purchased their homes. Some even had an expanding 401(k) about which to brag at family gatherings. Reverse assimilation, then, seemed the only fighting way forward.

Aiko had done her best. In the process, she lost her sense of safety.

Of all the things she had to fear, poverty and death by Night Marchers conquered all other prospects. She dreaded the flop of her literary career, just as she dreaded the rapping drumbeat, the low ringing of the pū, the chanting. Her tūtū's tales still rang orchestral in her ears all these years later. Her tūtū's guidance organized in her brain like an instruction manual:

- Once the moon has washed the night sky in light, go home. Avoid spending time outdoors in the evenings. Shutter all windows and ensure screens are fixed in place.
- Avoid frequenting sacred sites, including Kalama Valley, Kaʻena Point, Mokulēʻia, Kaniakapūpū, Haleakalā, Mauna Kea, or anywhere one may encounter bones of kānaka maoli.

- Pay attention to the lunar cycle: you will most often encounter them during Pō Kāne.
- Beware of torches, drumbeats, and the dissonant blow of the conch shell.
- If sighted by a Night Marcher, remove all your clothes and lie facedown.
- Consider peeing on yourself as a last resort.
- If you get that flopping-fish, stomach-as-a-fist, grit-in-the-teeth, tongue-like-a-stone sort of feeling—*run*.

Now tūtū was dead, and Aiko left to pen a very different tale by her lonesome.

But she needed time. Following the failure of her first book, Aiko had been reluctant to return to her fiction, lest she suffer the reality that she could no longer do the one thing at which she'd once achieved mediocrity. To feel her mind and her hand quite literally swept up in a gust of inspiration was an impossible gift. She rushed the drafting process, if only to prevent the gift from spiriting away. The Night Marchers, these deceased warrior spirits, lived in a robust vessel in her mind; her brain was rife with ideas. She wrote the first story in eight uninterrupted hours. The collection, in eight months.

Her Google search history was a single repetitious scroll of Night Marcher–related inquiries. Of course, no one had ever captured visual evidence of their Night Marcher encounters. Could you imagine, a spirit sloughing their sanctimonious skin and bearing their truth to a mortal? Instead, she scanned artistic rendering after rendering, observing Night Marchers depicted as championed Hawaiian warriors, their fists raised to the murky sky, malo stained a dazzling red not unlike the blood that licked the tips of the wooden spears they bore. She saw illustrations of Night Marchers more apparition than of this world, zombied creatures just wandering around, a translucent shell of themselves. In some search results, all she saw were torches, a whole waking row of them kindling the dark sky in streaks of light.

Now she had written the thing, had notified her agent of its completion as a first draft, had shared her enthusiasm with her husband the physicist. Though he maintained a perfunctory stance toward anything unrelated to physics, he perked up at the mention of Night Marchers. No, he hadn't heard of any fiction that explores this subject matter. Yes, he believed deeply that it would sell. Aiko, enthused by the praise, proceeded to phone several colleagues with the promising news. Expectations amassed in the ether. She closed her eyes and saw dollar signs but also book jackets, starred reviews, accolades, blurbs of high esteem. She saw her book earning out its advance, astonishing.

She hadn't seen her manuscript vibrating, a routine haunting. Must she tend to this phenomenon before any of her other dreams could come true?

★ ★ ★

THE NEXT MORNING, the morning of her panel discussion, Aiko woke to her manuscript pages scattered across the bedroom floor. The chaos pulled her to her knees. She tried to make sense of the dispersal, maybe tease a pattern from the clutter. But it was just a mess of pages, strewn across the beige carpet as if a mighty gust of wind had flown and alighted each sheet overnight.

Aiko tried her best to reorganize the pages, but the double-sided printing coupled with the fact that she'd overslept made the challenge ever more tedious, and after a few moments of expended labor, Aiko gave up. There would be plenty of time after the panel to clarify her life.

Aiko collected the pages, order be damned, and retired them to the binder before accelerating her morning routine. She would not arrive late to her first speaking engagement in months. Beneath the bitter hotel lights, Aiko applied tinted moisturizer and powder, she clabbered her eyelashes with black mascara and fitted her robust frame in a delicate ivory blouse. She deliberated: a skirt or dress pants? She peered through the smudged bedroom glass, saw spears of light piercing down on the sea of high-rises. The skirt swallowed her in its narrow, puckered maw.

She packed her purse with lightweights: her wallet, panel notes, the colleague's terrible memoir, a lighter, a bottle of water. Outside, the heat was a creature that settled on her shoulders. She smiled through it, pleased with her choice of wardrobe. She walked four steps and her knees buckled. It was happening more and more lately, as though her once sprightly, capable body were now rebelling against her brain's instructions like a surly teenager. Growing old was terrible, she decided, and she would need to hurry her book along before it fossilized her.

The Uber a good ten minutes away, Aiko settled on a hotel bench beside an angular white man in Dockers smoking a cigarette. She held her notecards in her left hand, her phone in her right. She did not look at the white man, and he didn't bother with her. They existed beneath a blanket of detached intimacy for several minutes, and then a drum rapped at the sky, sending ripples through hazy clouds and skylines, its reverberations grounding Aiko's bones. She heard it again—*rap, rap*. Her head swiveled left and right. Finally she looked at the white man, but he appeared unfazed.

Rap, rap. Rap, rap, rap, rap. The tempo she was unfamiliar with, but the drums themselves, that was the pounding pahu of her childhood. That was a Night Marcher sound.

She felt it then, the flopping-fish feeling taking root deep in her naʻau.

Then the Uber was pulling into the hotel's porte cochere, and Aiko quickly gathered her things and unfolded into the passenger seat. The pahu drumming ceased, as did the flopping-fish sensation. Silence molded around her. She exchanged pleasantries with the driver and skimmed through her notecards. Nothing she read in this moment would do her any good two hours from now, yet Aiko persisted. The driver, hazardously merging across three lanes, asked what she was doing in Austin.

"A writers' panel," she tried to explain. "At the university. People ask questions about our writing and process and such, and we try our best to answer them."

The driver asked what kind of writing was she talking about here—for the papers? The *Austin Chronicle*? He was a bit of a disciple to that paper. Sent in his fair share of op-eds and was even chummy with one of the sports editors. She clarified for him: fiction writing. She knew little about journalism and even less about sports, though his relationship to the editor sounded very lovely. But fiction writing was what this panel was slated to address; particularly, the role of place in fiction.

He muttered his *huhs* and *uh-huhs* then redirected his attention to the road ahead.

Aiko glanced down at her hands. She held her notecards firmly, and they did not buzz or hum or vibrate. She knew the sound she'd heard exploding through the sky was the sound of a pahu drum because of its sunken vibrancy and wide, guttural boom. She knew Night Marchers would be close by the sight of kindled torches and the hollow exhalation of the pū. She knew these things implicitly yet was incapable of explaining them to the driver or to anyone else.

AIKO, THE WRITER

For the duration of the drive, Aiko stared out the window and catalogued the city's trees, its sidewalks littered with scooters and electric bikes, its swanky glass constructions, and the harsh white skin of its people.

Eventually the car pulled up to a burnt-orange building where dozens of young and old people had amassed beside an ornate fountain. Aiko breathed heavily. As she stepped out of the car, the driver cleared his throat and wished her luck.

It wasn't until she was seated at the panel, flanked by an Odessan to her left and a Californian to her right, that Aiko realized the man had driven off with her notecards.

ACCORDING TO THE conference schedule, a wine and cheese reception was to follow Aiko's panel discussion. Yet given how poorly she viewed her performance on the panel, Aiko was reluctant to attend all future events related to this dreadful conference, much less a loose mingle where the wine would be silty and the cheese cubed and cheddar and melting. She called Pamela, whom she'd observed wincing in the audience, but got no answer. She called her husband the physicist but he could talk only for a few minutes, his lab's PI was in town and demanding of his time. She was desperate to talk to someone about the burning smell in that cardboard box of a room, the smell and the thud of pahu drums bleeding into her brain. Aiko was running out of people to call when a balding white man approached her beside the garish fountain, hoping to discuss her performance on the panel.

He reported her insights had given him a lot to think about, far more than those elicited by her fellow panelists. He was especially attuned to her musings on what it means to be an Indigenous writer writing for a white audience, despite the fact it seemed a significant departure from the topic at hand. Admittedly, he'd found her little panic over a nonexistent fire deeply unnerving, and the anecdote about her grandma's ghost exceedingly long and slightly alarming—from where he hailed, folks didn't subscribe to the existence of ghosts, and anyone who did was viewed as thick in the head—but he believed he understood the point she was attempting to make, however poorly.

He introduced himself as Jim, and said he was excited to get his hands on her upcoming collection.

Aiko shook his hand. She knew she had to remove herself from the fountain thronged with conference attendees, with the poor souls who'd endured her panic. Observing the many authorial clusters, she was acutely aware of her solitary stance, and how even the amiable white man had approached her but hesitantly. Quietly Aiko tugged away from the crowd and turned on her heels down West Twenty-First, passing undergrads in burnt-orange attire cupping coffees to their chests, passing graduate students appearing adrift and forlorn. One student in particular, a redhead haloed by enormous muffled headphones and with a face spotted with acne, grimaced at her in a way reminiscent of the Māori haka, the ferocity of visage thundering through her as she walked, and she walked on. As their paths intersected, Aiko peered over her shoulder. She saw the redhead embrace a bearded stranger, exchange a bro-like handshake before they grabbed each other by the shoulders. Aiko, exceedingly unnerved, walked on.

When she approached Guadalupe, Aiko heard the drums again. She passed through a Target, hoping the clerestory windows and insulated walls and significant display of capitalism might muffle the sound. Before leaving, she exchanged twelve dollars for a pack of tissues, a candy bar, and a singing magnet in the shape of Texas. It was a gift for her husband, the tissues and candy bar a gift for herself (though hell if she deserved it). Exiting the Target, Aiko was walloped by a gust of hot wind and the echoes of an oli with which she was familiar:

I ku mau mau
I ku wa
I ku mau mau
I ku hulu hulu
I ka lanawao
I ku wa
I ku wa huki
I ku wa ko

I ku wa a mau
A mau ka eulu
E huki, e
Kulia
Umia ka hanu
A lana ua holo ke akua

It was an invocation she remembered from her tūtū's tales, a call for kānaka maoli to pull together, to push forward as one lāhui. Aiko glanced all around her, probing for the source of the sound. But the bodies shrouding her were haole, Caucasian, white to the bone. She turned down Guadalupe and walked on.

I ku mau mau. I ku mau mau.

Tūtū had taught her the oli long ago. When tūtū was still alive, Aiko spent several evenings of her childhood and adolescence sleeping over at her home in Waikāne Valley. Though the 'āina on which the home was constructed was reputably haunted, Aiko had no trouble finding sleep at night, no trouble traversing unlit halls and the weedy yard through which tiny creatures traveled. She paced barefoot outside, she chewed on spears of fountain grass and a few times she gummed dirt. Tūtū delighted in watching her granddaughter roam feral. When she'd return home, Aiko's parents would balk.

"We don't eat dirt!" her mother would exclaim, pawing her daughter's face with cleaning wipes.

But Aiko felt entirely herself tucked inside the belly of O'ahu's windward side, eating grass and eating dirt, watching the sun and the stars bend around her. As a child, whenever she would hear the pahu drums, the "I Ku Mau" oli unfolding around her, Aiko would think it nothing more than Waikāne Valley showing off for the masses. The magic of the 'āina on full display. When the burning would tickle her nose, she'd think it was the neighbors roasting a pig.

The drums, chants, the burning, all made sense on O'ahu, where Night Marchers roamed regal and disquieting. It did not make sense in the landscape of the American South, yet the quicker Aiko paced down Guadalupe, the louder these sounds and smells vibrated inside her. A chill traveled up her back, ascending rung after rung of her delicate spine. She passed tentlike T-shirts parachuting tiny blonds, she passed several large dog breeds walking their otherwise aimless owners. One woman in particular, dressed in tie-dye and white sneakers, locked her in uneasy eye contact. When their paths crossed, Aiko inhaled the intensity of charred flesh, yet the woman appeared entirely intact. Her pale skin luminescent under the broiling heat. Aiko fled inside a bus shortly after, indifferent to its number or route.

At the second stop, Aiko took a call from Pamela, who was frustrated with her friend for neglecting the wine and cheese reception.

"So many people have questions for you! And they're asking *me*, because apparently we look alike. What is happening to you?"

Aiko had no idea what Pamela was talking about. She couldn't envision a world in which she and Pamela might be mistaken for each other.

Pamela wanted to know where her friend was in space.

Aiko glanced at the front of the bus for an indication of its route, but the way the old bus driver seemed to make direct eye contact with her through the front mirror was deeply unsettling, and so she returned her gaze to her own hand.

"I think I might be sick, or getting sick," Aiko said. "I'm very nauseous. I'm sorry to miss the reception."

Pamela wished her friend well then hung up. Aiko got off at the next stop. Her attempt to center herself by gazing skyward was a miserable failure, and Aiko nearly stumbled off the sidewalk and sprawled into an open road. She didn't. She found her footing, found comfort against a telephone pole battered with missing-pet posters. She just needed to rest her eyes for a few minutes. Ten minutes, max. Traveling and public speaking and being haunted by Night Marchers was exhausting. All she needed to return to herself was a brief rest.

AND IN THIS brief rest, Aiko found her tūtū. She had returned once again as a moʻo, which was alarming,

AIKO, THE WRITER

since moʻo were nonexistent in Austin, Texas. But here was the moʻo nonetheless, her gummy pads of digits finding purchase on the telephone pole just above Aiko's head, her eyes buggy and capricious. Aiko knew she had disappointed her tūtū, that one day she would pay for her hewa creation, this terrible collection. She reached toward the telephone pole to touch the moʻo, but the thing crawled away before she could make contact.

I told you what to do, and you did not listen to me.

Aiko nodded.

I told you there are ways to tell Hawaiian stories and ways to make Hawaiian stories vulnerable to the white hand.

Yes, you did.

I told you to be extremely careful with your choices.

Aiko swallowed a sob, jagged and unwieldy as a chunk of coral.

Honor the kapu. Do not write about what you cannot write about.

I am so sorry, Aiko said. I don't know what you want me to do.

But then the moʻo was just a moʻo, and of course she couldn't talk.

AIKO, THE WRITER, is leaving for Oʻahu today. She has fulfilled her commitments in Austin, Texas, and is now released to her homeland. Kulāiwi. Where the bones of her ancestors are buried. Where her tūtū, enraged, still roams.

In the hotel room, Aiko returns to the shower but now the water is cold, far too cold, most would call it frigid. She can barely shampoo without shrieking aloud. Stepping onto a floor mat, dripping icy beads, palming her mouth, shivering. She changes into comfy clothes and disregards the mascara, the creamy primer and the powder. She packs haphazardly. The manuscript, its pages still out of order, is a wrangled animal confined to her binder. She will not touch it again, she vows right there in that icebox of a hotel room, though perhaps back home she will give it a proper burial. She will trust her tūtū has her best interests at heart, that this is no longer some routine haunting. Something else her tūtū once said: *Do not question the words of our lāhui. Do not question the gods who are very much alive.* But Aiko never did believe in any gods.

Aside from the constancy of drumming, the smells of fire, the muffled echoes of an oli from her childhood, aside from her indistinct impression that she is floating underwater or being chased or being watched, Aiko's return trip proves more or less uneventful. She manages to catch an Uber within a few minutes of placing her request, and her flight is on time. No delays through security, no issues with boarding. The plane lands twenty minutes early. While taxiing, Aiko rummages through her bag to locate her manuscript. To hold those vibrating pages in her hands one last time. But her binder is empty, the pages gone. Aiko swallows a tremendous lump, sends it down her throat.

AIKO, THE WRITER

While waiting for the pilot to turn off the seat belt sign, Aiko switches her phone off airplane mode and dials her husband. He doesn't answer, so she tries again. Still no answer. Aiko presses her skull into the inflexible headrest and makes to sleep. If the manuscript is no longer with her, perhaps her luck has changed. She is still moderately young; there is still time to salvage her career as a writer. She can articulate another story, equally Indigenous yet not ringed by a kapu. She scans the plane for a moʻo or any sign of her tūtū, but this is a sterile environment, and of course she is alone here.

The seat belt sign clicks off, and passengers scramble to their feet, vying to open the overhead compartments first and fastest. She has never understood what compels people to dash off planes like that. Aiko remains in her seat until everyone has passed, their grumbles and gabs muted by the resounding blast of pahu drums in her head. She sits until a handsome flight attendant asks her to please deboard the plane. She sits, because it is a very strange season in her life to return home, and because she has soiled her seat with urine.

ENDING A STORY is no easy feat. Mostly, none of Aiko's stories close in a clean, pretty, satisfying package. The only pure story in her draft collection is the one inspired by her tūtū's life on Molokai, the one in which Night Marchers are curiously nonexistent and no one dies. It is a terrible thing, to end a story with finality. Possibly it is Aiko's greatest realized fear.

Instead, Aiko would like to end her tales with torches. With the rhythmic rattle of pahu drums and the oli of her childhood. She would like to end the story dreaming. Or just waking up. No, dreaming. That syrupy slip of time in which consciousness is shelved beneath the desires and the demons of the mind. The Night Marchers are not demons. They are deceased, and they are phenomenally strong. Years and years later, when they finally come for her, Aiko won't even be surprised. Her literary career downright luminescent, Aiko will be a household name, and she will die in her home. She will open her arms to the Night Marchers' heat, their violence and power, and she will consider herself impossibly special. It is the only way her story can end.

But Aiko isn't special, and neither are her stories. Her plane taxis, her suitcase trundles down the concourse, her husband retrieves her. Back home, she sloughs her clothes and lazes in the tub, lukewarm water lapping at her brown skin. She cannot believe she peed herself on the plane. She tries not to think of that now. For now all is well, except for that flopping-fish, stomach-as-a-fist, grit-in-the-teeth, tongue-like-a-stone sort of feeling, walloping her, drowning her. Underwater, she can't hear her own thoughts over the resounding drums, and she can no longer taste, no longer smell anything but the smoldering of torches doused in light.

Some Things I Know About Elvis

There were many instances when I should have paid closer attention to signs, but never more so than when I found myself lost in the Royal Hawaiian Hotel. I tell this to Sara; we are sitting at a bar without a name, and I'm trying to get her to come home with me. She asks what was so wrong with being stranded in the Pink Lady, and I tell her there was an Elvis Presley impersonator guarding the entrance, asking passersby for a cigarette.

"I don't understand," she says, and I try to explain myself but then our drinks arrive. Tanqueray and tonic for Sara, a li hing margarita on the rocks for me. We prop our elbows on the sticky vinyl bar top, not looking at each other. The stools are peeling chrome. No back support. The li hing is sour, like a burst blood vessel in my throat. Always I am thinking of local kine tidbits to share with Sara, but Sara isn't interested. She comes here every summer, brings her kānaka hair into the same Mōʻiliʻili bar in search of a good time. They treat her like ʻohana here, and I am supremely jealous; Sara's got the blood even though I've lived here in Hawaiʻi all my life.

The bar is feathered with dark wood, wet lacquer floors, fringed antique furniture. We meet here every summer like old friends, even though neither of us is all that old and Sara isn't very friendly. It began five years prior at my invitation, and despite our questionable chemistry and really not having all that much to talk about, we've maintained the tradition ever since.

She's so quiet and interior, this Sara. I try to peel back her reservations gradually, so as not to spook her off. I tell Sara the whole thing started because I was looking for someone to love, but she wants to know more about the Elvis Presley impersonator.

"Bad breath. Ashy, cigarette-y breath. Though he seemed to be having trouble procuring one."

Her face scrunches in confusion. "I don't see the problem. Do you hate Elvis or something?"

This proves a difficult question to answer, so instead I press on.

"Lucky for him I show up, I always keep a pack of Kools in any purse I carry." And to taunt her, I pull out a pack from the back pocket of my denim tote, leave it charged on the bar top between us.

"My father smoked those," Sara muses.

I smile. "So anyway, I give him a cigarette, right? But instead of asking me for a light, he goes and turns to the guy to his right, and—you'll never believe it."

"What? *What?*"

"That guy was an Elvis Presley impersonator *too*! And the guy next to him, and the guy behind him . . ."

The Presleys, I explain, had assembled for the first annual International Elvis Presley Impersonator Conference, an intimate gathering of two-hundred-plus actors from around the globe. They were taking over the place, a nuisance, like the crawl of mucus congestion in someone who's also dying. Each one had committed their life to the same dozen or so singles crooned by the late King of Rock 'n' Roll. Most of the songs you'll remember from *Lilo & Stitch*, I say, though she's never seen the film.

"You wouldn't believe how many ways there are to impersonate the same person. All these short men wearing platform shoes, tall men crouching and stooping their shoulders to make themselves smaller. They all had his slicked-back quiff, so black and gelled, almost wet-looking. It was hard to look at them for a long time without wanting to kill myself."

Someone toys with the stereo, spilling a coil of fuzzy sound through the dank hall.

Sara likes this story. Her back is fixed straight like a doorway I could walk through. Beside her, my posture is poor. Sara's father, the Kools smoker, wasn't an Elvis impersonator but he was a lifelong fan of the King's music. Some called him committed, others labeled him obsessed. Last we spoke, Sara told me he'd named their childhood dog Presley, the frigid outdoor cat Elvis.

Every summer, I gather new data about the family through our brief bar exchanges. We met at this very bar, where we blottoed our brains on Big Island Iced Teas and I held her hair while she puked like crazy on the parking lot asphalt then convinced her to exchange numbers. Sara intrigued me. Sara's father also wasn't kānaka but held all the passion for the culture her own native mother resented. Sara is a muddied in-between, composited and slick like spilled motor oil. Her last name is Watanabe. Her father's name was Milton.

I tell her I met another Elvis impersonator in the Pink Lady's basement lounge. I was meant to be on a date in Waikīkī with a man I'd met online but couldn't find my way to the restaurant. (I avoid the tourist trap of town every chance I get.) The Elvis in the lounge was wide and pudgy, too short despite wearing three-inch white boots to appear even remotely convincing. Also he was Japanese like me, so the whole big hulking white-boy masquerade wasn't really adding up. Still, I liked his eyes. The hook-shaped scar tattooed over his left thumb. He reminded me of my brother, an easygoing fisherman with the same kind eyes. The lounge crooned a smooth, velvety jazz, so different from the whimsical Hawaiian tunes that washed through the hotel's corridors.

This man's name was Kit. As in sewing, as in survival.

I bought Kit's drink. If I'm being honest, it's this thing I do. Buy them their drinks and make them feel accommodated by the youngest girl in the bar.

It worked, with Kit. He seemed blue, as blue as his Blue Hawaiian beverage. I asked him if he knew where I could find the Doraku sushi bar, but he wasn't from around here. Boise, he informed me. I hadn't asked where he was from, but then I had to wonder—what does an Asian kid in Boise want from the King of Rock 'n' Roll?

I asked what his favorite Elvis song was. "That's Someone You Never Forget," but I'd never heard it before.

IF I'M BEING honest, I don't have a brother. I've just always wanted one.

SARA DOESN'T INTERRUPT my story, but I can tell she's withered away to restlessness. Her hands tear at the sopping cocktail napkin, her eyes glass over like the sea. So fine, I'm bad at telling stories. Can't get to the point fast enough and then when I do it's all inflated surprise, shock and awe, nothing special. I order her another Tanqueray and tonic from a bartender who looks like Steve McGarrett, the '70s version tapered down by those austere forehead wrinkles and a slight frame. She seems surprised by my presumption.

"Don't you feel accommodated?" I ask her.

Sara says mostly she feels tired. She bunches the cocktail napkin into tiny little balls and arranges them in order of size. A curious odor suffuses her clothes, something stale and dried out. Supposedly, she's here to handle her father's estate, except she doesn't know any of his passwords. Ten years prior, this wouldn't have been an issue. She says her father wanted all his money to go to founding Hawai'i's first interactive museum dedicated to the memory of the late Elvis Presley. Her mother wants to keep the money for herself. Her brother wants peace in the family; he's young, fragile, easily frazzled. Sara wants to return to Boston, where no one even knows she is Hawaiian or what that could possibly mean. Where she doesn't have to answer any prodding questions, because there's no one around to ask them.

The entire bar heaves around us. I ask if she'd like to get out of here, but Sara says no. So I return to the Elvis impersonator, because really Sara has dumped quite a load on me and for all my many talents, comforting others is not one of them.

I say this Elvis, this Japanese imposter, can't believe I've never heard "That's Someone" before. "So he starts to hum it. Right there in the middle of this bougie jazz lounge. And then he starts to sing. Like this."

I sway whimsically on the stool and I sing: "When she is far away / You'll think of her each day . . ."

I LIKE TO picture Sara reaching for my hand, clearing her throat, singing. Sara and me, tone-deaf, singing together. Making something special. Just because it won't happen doesn't mean I can't invent the nostalgia for it in my head. The mental gymnastics through which I can tumble would absolutely astound you.

"SO, YOU SLEPT with him." Sara would like me to get to the point. But that's the thing—whatever is the point?

I tell her I didn't sleep with him. I kissed him on the forehead. Then I ran out of there as fast as I could.

"You're such a strange little thing," she says. A drop in her cadence then, like if we stay here any longer, something might happen.

"I didn't sleep with him," I say.

What I did was keep running. I ran through the Pink Lady's gilded halls, its oppressively Moorish design and the rogue rumble of luggage that bounced off the bowled ceilings. I ran under the vaulted coral archways and out onto the porte cochere until I could see the exterior's pink plaster veneer, its blue-tiled roof. Until a valet attendant dressed exorbitantly approached me with his crooked tie and empty hands, asking me if everything was okay. I held his hands. But here's the thing. When I glanced back at him, he looked exactly like an Elvis impersonator. Same hair, same snarled lip and platform boots. Same swagger. I was holding hands with one of the Presleys.

Sara snorts so bad she sends her drink bubbling over her face. So bad I flag down the McGarrett look-alike, ask for a fistful of napkins. He hands us two.

She reaches for the napkins but I hold them close. Scrunch them like wilted flower petals and bring them to my chest. I press a wedge of napkin to Sara's lips. Pouty things, painted a subtle shade of terra-cotta. I brush the napkin and then my fingers over her lips. Sara stays very still, that porcelain posture I've perfected in my head.

Sara. Every summer I wait for her, sinking into my own elastic skin. My heart a rotten, worm-bitten fruit. I lose jobs, friends, entire fresh lives waiting for her. I hope she'll call, hope she won't lose interest or my number. I peel flakes of dead skin from my cuticles and picture her face pressed against my floorboards. The backdrop of my awful fringed curtains behind her tapestry of dark curls. I think of her father. I make magic in my mind; see what I can do.

I continue. "At that point I figured I was just going crazy, or the whole online dating thing was a doomed venture and I should just go home. And I was nearly out of the porte cochere when I realized: I left my wallet at the lounge."

Intentionally, she accuses, but I am insistent.

"I'm just naturally careless."

"Me too, though I'm starting to lose the point of this story." She is now rummaging through her purse, a little black square ribbed with leather tassels. Looking for her car keys, maybe, and a spark of fear clips onto my spine. But she just needed a mirror.

"The point is . . . I'm getting to that. But you have to understand how many of them there were."

Because it wasn't just the valet or Kit the crooner, it was the whole hotel now. The guests wearing his snug white jumpsuits bejeweled in shiny gems, the boutique workers cloaked behind his signature angular collars. The haole children folded into keiki copies of the red aloha shirt he wore in *Blue Hawaii*. Was it strange I was hoping to find the dying, bloated version of him wandering the halls? Of course, they only wanted the King at his prime. I rode the elevator sandwiched between two Presleys who reeked of Lenel for Men. They sandwiched me and I thought I might pass out, might require resuscitation from an Elvis impersonator. When the bell struck and the doors spit us out into the basement, one of the Presleys told me, "Have a nice night now." A cluster of five or so Presleys of varying heights lingered outside the elevator doors, laughing.

Kit was still planted in the lounge.

"Back for more tunes?" he asked me. And around us, tiny cocktail tables dotted by the hunched backs of Presleys. The bartender was a Presley, too, and how had I not noticed that before?

I had to know. Was there anyone staying at the hotel who wasn't a Presley?

He said, "I think the word you're looking for is *infestation*."

SOME THINGS I like about Sara: her smile, the flutter in her eyes, her stubby fingers, the knots in her hair, the stories she tells (particularly those about her father), the pidgin accent she can't shake.

SOME THINGS I know about Elvis: He visited Hawaiʻi first in November 1957 and twenty years later for the last time before his death; he passed far too many hours drinking at the Ala Wai Yacht Harbor; he drove the braided bends of Tantalus; he spooned through cans of Bumble Bee tuna. In a telegram to the *Star-Bulletin*, Elvis wrote: *ALOHA VERY ENJOYABLE TRIP SUNBATHING SWIMMING TENNIS READING I KNOW I WILL ENJOY YOUR ISLANDS LIKE TO SURF AND SWIM GETTING GOOD TAN ON BOARD HAVE READ ABOUT HAWAIIAN*

HOSPITALITY AND AM EAGERLY LOOKING FORWARD TO SAME BEST OF LUCK ELVIS PRESLEY

But he never stayed at the Royal Hawaiian. The "Heartbreak Hotel" was the Ilikai.

THEN KIT THE Presley listed some things he liked about me: My straight hair, and how nice I smelled. The way I kept coming back for more. How I bought his drink and made him feel accommodated. He started to hum "That's Someone" again, but I'd already forgotten how the song went.

Kit said, "You know, Elvis wrote that song about his mother. Some people think it was meant for Priscilla, but that's not right. He loved his mother most in the entire world."

"Mothers are great," I said. It was a stupid thing to say. Not even sure I believed it.

I guess I'd settled into things, at that point, because Kit ordered me a drink from the bartending Presley, and if I was telling the truth, I really didn't know much about mothers, knew even less about fathers because I hadn't had one since my tenth year when my own father left the house one morning for a shift with his construction crew and never came back. My mother resumed the washing of rice, slinging trash bags over her shoulder, scrubbing the floors of grime, spilled tea. She seemed unfazed, so

I assumed I should be, too. Sometimes fathers disappear and that's just life and life is okay.

Sara, with no semblance of cocktail napkins left to dismantle, has resorted to tugging the skin around her cuticles, shearing them clear of the finger and leaving behind soft, pinked tissue. I'm scared I am reminding her of her father. All the Presleys remind me of my father because supposedly he was a superfan, though I didn't know him long enough to see the fixation for myself. I know he attended a handful of Elvis tribute shows because there are these pictures of him, his arm wrapped around a bunch of white suits, his face glowing. I also know of his other 'ohana, the one he made after he left us, because my mother told me. First came the girl, then the brother, the one I never had. Sara says her father was also a superfan, though I already knew this. We speak every summer about her father and still I don't know how to tell her.

Sara asks if I can tell her how things ended with the Presleys, but the truth is, they're still there. Kit called it an *infestation*. I don't know if I would go that far, but how to explain the fact that it's been nearly three months and the Presleys haven't left yet? No conference lasts that long, and anyway, the bellhops and valets, the bartenders and the concierge and those curious little men at check-in, they're all dressed as Presleys. I've been back a few times since that whole getting-lost fiasco, walked the coral halls and waved to grown men playing dress-up. No one is talking about the infestation. They're just always there now.

Sara softens. "I sorta like that," she says. "Like a bunch of tired old men found peace there and just stayed. That's nice to think about."

What I think about are their families. What of the bitter wives or husbands left staring at the stove, counting hours and then days, months? What of the children they left behind?

A kink in the stereo, then, and someone has started playing "Don't Be Cruel." This might be the sign I've been waiting for, or else an easy reason to leave this damn bar. Finally. I flag down the bartender, ask to close out my tab. The air here is saturated with something wet and alive, and I watch goose bumps rise off my forearms. Sara says that's probably a good idea, she's stayed too late anyway. Tomorrow she'll meet with her mother and the executor of her father's will to discuss Next Steps, and maybe in five years when she returns for summer break there will be the Elvis Presley Museum operating somewhere on Hawaiian soil, possibly at the Royal Hawaiian. Or maybe her mother will be rich. Impossible to say, because things never go the way you think they will.

I scribble my signature on the receipt, curl my fingers to hide evidence of my name. But Sara isn't looking at the receipt. She's staring at my face, then, and I am whopped sideways thinking of how she might perceive me. The pale complexion, the yanking wrinkles around my eyes, my lips, the textured rise of blackheads pimpling my nose. It is humiliating to list the ways I have prepared for this meeting, so I won't do it. I will pocket my wallet and sobriety and walk a few paces behind Sara as we exit the bar. She'll start whistling, and I'll brush up really close to her and explain how dangerous it is to whistle at night, how the sound attracts Night Marchers. She'll stare at her feet contemplatively and say, "Huh, I didn't know that," and I will have taught her something new about her culture. I'll let her guide me along the sidewalk, through the parking lot, and when I ask her if she'd like to come home with me, she will say yes. So easy. She'll follow behind me through traffic lights and stop signs in her sad rental car, and when we get to my place, I will bring my lips to her face as we linger in the doorway; *see what I can do.* I will sing into her hair: "And you know she'll wait for you / That's someone you never forget . . ."

I'LL TELL HER the truth about her father, *our* father, who left the house one morning for a shift with his construction crew and never came back.

★ ★ ★

I'LL WRECK HER whole life with the truth—*see what you made me do.* It's dangerous, really, being so in love with someone you'll never forget.

OR I'LL LET her sleep. Watch the rise and fall of her chest, listen for the rap of exhalations, snores, or other signs of life. I won't be cruel, won't touch her, but I'll let her rest for the night in my bed so she can sleep off all those drinks. I'll lie beside her. I'll let her sleep. I'll dream of the Presleys and their two lives: the playing-pretend version, and the men they really are, the ones they'd rather forget. In my dreams they have permanently infested the Royal Hawaiian, and I live there, too, roam the halls alongside hundreds of Presleys and their flared-leg jumpsuits, their energetic penny loafers. I don't have to see Sara to know she is living there, too.

Touch Me Like One of Your Island Girls: A Love Story

*WANTED: ISLAND GIRL
DARK HAIR, BROWN SKIN,
PIDGIN ACCENT.
Compensation is commensurate with experience and
negotiable. Role to be filled ASAP.*

But Mehana wasn't even all that brown anymore. If anything, she pulled more Japanese, the ligature of her mixed blood taming her Hawaiian roots, her time on the mainland bleaching her skin to a clabber. Such a shame she'd gone broke, a shame she'd returned home and needed the money now, when she'd only just aged past her prime and couldn't even flaunt the beach bronze that'd once defined her youth.

An abundance of shame to sit with, these days.

These days, Mehana was also coming to terms with her inability to orgasm. Never not once had she encountered this problem in the past. So long as her massage wand was fully charged and her jalousie windows cinched shut, Mehana could guarantee her body a significant curtain call of pleasure at least once a night. What with her gymnastic fingers and the tools tucked away in her underwear drawer, reaching at least one erogenous zone was no trouble, while blended orgasms were frequent. Now she was spending over two hundred dollars, two weeks' pay, on something called a rabbit head vibrator.

What made her no-orgasm condition a particular bummer is she had started seeing someone. An awkward, shaggy-browed hapa with an ungraspable personality. His name was Katsutoshi, but out of respect to his predominantly haole colleagues, he went by Karl. Karl with a *K*. Mehana found his whitened name absurd. She was also suspicious of people who worked in cybersecurity. But Karl was the first man to show her any interest in who knows how long, and Mehana was tired of subsisting on a cheap diet of tortilla chips and Pace salsa, of sulking off to bed at nine P.M. every night with a pillow wedged between her thighs, alone.

To her dismay, Mehana learned on their fourth date that Karl was a federal hire who didn't make much more than she did as an office manager. Around the same time, she stopped having orgasms. Film and television had groomed her for this very moment—the transition to faking orgasms with a partner. But goodness, she was barely in her thirties—could it really happen this early? And would she ever recover from such a terrible ailment?

She liked to think yes. She was trying. But work at Gina's Talent Agency was keeping her later and later, zapping her consciousness and wringing her out. Her long-dormant dream of becoming a famous screenwriter-director had accumulated a mess of cobwebs. As for Karl, she hadn't seen him in days. Then it was the first day of spring—a new beginning!—and Mehana was rising from bed with one hand groping inside her underwear, determined to reorient the direction of the swerving tanker that had become her life.

The first day of spring, and Mehana ran into her old friend Patti Tanabe. Each of them had stopped at Aliʻi Coffee en route to their respective jobs—Mehana to Gina's studio, Patti to the downtown branch of Get Wild Productions. The women hadn't seen each other since those uneasy years post-college. Now they were both working in the entertainment industry, living out their aspirations but on largely different canvases. They made eye contact near the condiments counter, honi'd and embraced. Patti cinched the peach arms of her flannel cover-up around her waist, a lazy complement to her otherwise couture outfit. A cleft between her breasts was showing, and Mehana tried terribly hard not to think about that bare skin, and the skinscape she'd observed in Patti's recent sex video.

Instead, Mehana smiled and stayed. She decided Gina could spare her for thirty minutes, at least. Friendships were invaluable, even charged ones between women who hadn't spoken in over a decade.

Lazing around a tottering high-top, the women diced the past decade into digestible bites. Patti had married a haole, of course, and took up adult ballet lessons, which was surprising, for she'd never been all that flexible. Mehana told her about working as an office manager for Gina's studio, glamorizing the job perks while alluding to climbing the rungs, ascending the echelons, blah blah blah. She didn't talk about the miserable pay, or the slow accumulation of debt the way one accumulates trash magazines on a coffee table. Instead, she told Patti about Karl. *It's new*, was how she described it. Patti said her husband's name was Kevin.

They continued this shallow and circuitous chitchat until the early-morning hour burned out and Mehana could curtail her curiosity no longer: she needed to know about Get Wild Productions. How this girl she'd once shared a toothbrush with for two weeks in Galway, who used to have Bruddah Iz's "Hawai'i '78" programmed as her ringtone, could now stomach day after day working for a contemptible lowlife like Landon Wilder. (Though she didn't dare ask about *that* video.) If she was being honest, Mehana could care less about her friend's well-being and more about the man himself—how he took his coffee, how he could sleep at night. How could she?

"It's tough," Patti admitted with loose shoulders and a rounded, thick sigh. "And I don't wanna make excuses with you. He's a loser, no question. But I've started to think of the job as a way to champion Hawaiian rights."

Mehana sipped from her lukewarm latte, sending a splash of liquid down the wrong pipe. She coughed wildly. Patti offered her a napkin.

"Sorry," she said. "I don't think I understand."

"It's a bit of a circuitous route, I know. But did you ever think about the kānaka ʻōiwi wāhine he's employing for his projects? We've already moved past the foolishness of demeaning sex workers. Why can't we make this shift for our own cultural heritage?"

Mehana, always bristling at conflict, practiced a thoughtful nod. She did not want to be another woman in competition with her own kind.

"I know folks are all up in arms over this white dude making bank on Hawaiian stereotypes and our bodies and all that, but honestly? I'm doing fairly well for myself, too. He's not like other bosses, you know? He shares his profits. And he's nice, even to the janitors."

"I'm happy for you."

But they couldn't just sit there all day, nodding politely at each other. There was work to be done, orgasms to fashion, bosses to please. There was mail to sort and contracts to file, and there was certainly no time to waste diddling on a cell phone, though on their way out of Aliʻi,

Patti was doing just that, tapping away on an unseen keyboard while Mehana waited in the doorway awkwardly, absorbing the whiplash of cars speeding across South Beretania, glancing at her watch. The air was stale and stagnant, infected with bursts of sour gasoline and bus exhaust. They were both running very late.

After some time passed, Patti pocketed her cell phone just as Mehana's hummed in her purse. The women hugged and honi'd. Made half-hearted promises about future pau hana drinks, beach days, and double dates with their partners. Mehana hoped Patti spoke sincerely, for she was terribly lonely. She liked to think friendships, like any other ambition prone to spoiling, could be salvaged with time, effort, and attention from both parties. She was exceedingly optimistic, even without her orgasms.

As the women prepared to part ways, Patti extended one hand to her friend's shoulder. "I sent you an email, but don't feel any pressure to go through with it. It's just that I know Gina's pay is shit—I worked there for two months."

Of course she had. No matter how many rungs Mehana climbed, echelons she ascended, Patti would always supersede her. It was the central nature of their friendship.

Patti turned away, clacking her heels in departure, and immediately Mehana fished her phone from her purse to check the email. It was a list of jobs available at

Get Wild Productions. She read through the ads, and then she walked the four blocks to her office, absently gnawing the insides of her cheeks until she drew blood.

IT'S TRUE THAT Get Wild Productions and especially Landon Wilder were two of the most corrupt entities on island. It's also true that Gina's Talent Agency could only afford to pay Mehana minimum wage despite her three years of loyalty. She tried not to fault Gina—the economy tanked, Hawaiʻi's cost of living reached its apex—but when her boss strolled into the office well after ten wearing stiletto Louboutins and driving a company-leased Lexus GX, Mehana's resolve to think the best of her went as tepid as tap water.

Still, she stayed. Five going on six years of menial secretary labor, and Mehana never bothered to look for work elsewhere. Her Japanese parents couldn't fathom why she'd chosen to settle in this work. How much in loans had the government saddled her with just to afford her fancy East Coast college, where she studied, of all things, English and film? And now, six years postgrad and still working for the same talentless talent agency.

Now, traipsing through Fort Street Mall in Payless heels that sawed into the sides of her feet, Mehana imagined herself cast in roles daring, eager, and othered. She strolled past a hovel of particularly disheveled unhoused women, fingering cigarette rods and tweezing their hair, and pictured her own punchy spirit lounging in their shoes. Passing an Asian woman in beige slacks, walking at a fast clip and speaking frantically into her phone, Mehana imagined her own hands wrapped around that phone while she issued sharp commands to her lowly assistant: *Buy stocks! Cancel my appointments!* She could just as easily slip into the body of the Longs cashier, or of the Aliʻi Coffee barista who'd frothed her milk that morning. For so long her racial ambiguity had been a burden—this imprecise melding of Hawaiian, Japanese, an amalgam of white. But hapa girls were becoming less and less common, particularly in the talent industry, and Gina Figueroa, a hapa blend herself, was committed to championing girls of ambiguity, just as her career had been championed so many decades ago. It was only right to afford the same heartfelt charity to her longtime secretary, no?

Gina hadn't received many applicants after the ad for office manager first published. Mehana didn't interview. So long as she knew how to make coffee and agreed to the agency dress code (slacks every day and a modest amount of cleavage), Mehana had the job. She accepted the position enthusiastically, and between filing client offers and faxing contracts, she passed the time dreaming of writing screenplays, directing big-budget films in locales as foreign as Athens or as drab and lackluster as Fort Wayne, Indiana. Didn't matter where, really. So long as she could travel, explore, flee from the rock on which she'd floated, detached and unmoored, for the duration of her short life. Gina's Talent Agency was as good a place as any to begin.

Far better, she figured, than Get Wild Productions. While Mehana held no disdain for legitimate adult talent agencies, she couldn't accommodate Landon Wilder into her otherwise boundless tolerance for things taboo. A direct descendent of William Wilder, one of the many white men complicit in detaining Queen Liliʻuokalani before bankrolling the resulting territory, Landon was a true, unapologetic fuck. Blue eyes, blond hair, broad shoulders, and skin browned by immense beachfront leisure and the occasional spray tan. She knew where he worked (the penthouse suite of Executive Center, overlooking the unhoused and hungry, and the lolling currents of the Pacific Ocean), knew his beverage of choice at Aliʻi Coffee (quad-shot cappuccino with extra foam). She'd hated him for years and followed him around like a tracking hound, desperate to understand him, eager to slit his throat or suck him off. She couldn't make sense of it, this marriage of lust and loathing, though maybe this was the way things had always been, and only now was Mehana old enough to see the bleakness for herself.

Approaching the arm of Fort Street Mall, Mehana stared down the tumultuous face of her morning decision: to return to her little desk at her little job or to flee. To where, she couldn't say. But the dilemma met her there at the edge of Fort Street, morning after morning, year after year. She couldn't escape it, this drive to be absolutely anywhere else. She checked her phone.

*WANTED: ISLAND GIRL
DARK HAIR, BROWN SKIN,
PIDGIN ACCENT.
Compensation is commensurate with experience and negotiable. Role to be filled ASAP.*

But her pidgin was terrible.

In the email, Patti had highlighted a call for a talent publicity assistant, subordinate to Get Wild Productions' senior acquisitions agent. A salaried job, with full benefits and opportunities for career advancement. She skipped it and returned to the listing for an Island Girl then sent those cheap heels clacking down Fort Street in the direction from which she came.

THE ARTIFICIAL CHIME of a bell, and a woman who was more attractive than Landon Wilder greeted her in the lobby of Get Wild Productions. Sharp nose, red hair, accentuated coal eyebrows. She asked Mehana how she might be of assistance.

"My friend, Patti Tanabe . . ." Mehana pulled out her phone and attempted to scroll through her emails. "I'm here for the Island Girl audition?"

"Oh. You're early!"

"Sorry."

The woman waved her off. "It's nice to see an actress so punctual. Here." A shuffling of papers, then the woman presented Mehana with a pile of forms pinned to a matte black clipboard. "Skip the social security part, we don't need that. But do make sure you give us your current address. We'll send some complimentary stickers."

Mehana thanked her then sat in a too-soft armchair to review the forms. She surveyed the office. Glass walls, olive marbled tiles, silver ceiling of punctured tin. Across the room, frosted glass doors flanking the cryptic studio entrance. Both exceedingly extravagant and disappointing. She had pictured neons, fluorescents, furniture carved in daring and organic shapes found only in the forest's wet heart. Instead, there were coffee tables bracketed by hard edges, and a receptionist's desk that looked more or less like her own.

In between scribbling and surveying, Mehana checked her watch and phone repeatedly. In the years of working at Gina's, she had taken only two sick days and a two-week vacation when her parents invited her on their annual trip to Shinjuku. Otherwise, her attendance record was untarnished. She couldn't imagine Gina or any of her blond minions opening the doors without Mehana stationed properly in reception. Yet Gina had neither called nor emailed. She glanced again at her watch. 9:22 A.M.

She returned what she hoped was completed paperwork to the receptionist. "Sorry, I think I got my times mixed up. When exactly is the audition scheduled for?"

"Ten thirty, dear. You have so much time! Can I get you something to drink? Coffee, water, tea? We've got green, black, and herbal."

"I'm fine, thank you." Though she was thirsty, parched. She clenched her thighs together, ran her fingers over the charcoal stitching of her slacks. Her face burned at the ugly paisley top she'd fished from the bottom of her dresser that morning because she'd run out of quarters for laundry. She didn't own an iron; she'd smoothed the wrinkles with her palms as best she could. She imagined the women behind those frosted glass doors scanning her from top to bottom, snickering at her flyaways, her homely slacks coated in white lint, this awful top.

Then, a gust of artificial air ballooned her blouse. Startled, she looked up, and there was Landon Wilder—sandy blond curls, a significant tan, dimples punctuating his clownish grin—offering forth his Omega-watch-strapped wrist and inviting her to shake his hand.

It was his left hand. A gleaming gold band nearly half an inch thick strangled his wedding finger. She reached out and shook it. So a stupid woman had made him her husband.

"So good to meet you," he said.

This, the second disappointment: what a shrill and squeamish voice! After watching his broadcast interviews and listening to his ads on the radio, Mehana couldn't disentangle the posturing actor from this tenor-toned man standing before her in a terrible plum necktie. She felt the enormity of a hard lump ascending the rungs of her throat. How she wished for a drink—really any drink!—to dissolve this swelling node and right her. But it was far too late to make such a request to the receptionist, and even if it weren't, how might she maneuver around this massive, smiling man looming over her?

She swallowed repeatedly. Landon thanked her for showing up early, for actresses are rarely so punctual. "We won't get started with the audition until the other girls show up, but I wondered if you might like a tour of the studio while you wait."

As he spoke, Mehana took note of his teeth—tinged with biofilm yellow and accented by a noticeable gap between his upper front teeth. Mehana shared a similar gap, and had read somewhere about the condition, called midline diastema, and how it often reflected poor early behaviors such as extended pacifier use, thumb sucking, and the vaguely erotic "tongue thrusting." Afterward, she'd stood in front of a mirror, pushing her tongue back and forth against the bulwark of her front teeth, thinking, *Thrust, thrust.* Still, she was unaroused.

"Yes," she said now, tonguing her own queer gap. "That would be great."

MEHANA HAD LEARNED of the Island Girls after watching a clip of her old friend Patti spreading her asshole for a grievously sunburnt man to enter it. *Was the sunburn part of the shtick?* she wondered while the video continued to play. And did Patti choose to go full Brazilian, rather than sporting the elegant bush she'd honed all through high school and college? Mehana had always admired that bush, took comfort in its audacity and how closely it resembled the unkempt fur she'd let flourish between her legs.

Along with Patti's waxed vagina, there were her toned, tapered thighs, and her chest taped down by a clattering of halved coconuts, gutted of their meat and held together with green twine. Her traditional light-auburn locks were dyed an intrusive brown, almost black, and someone must have teased her hair to get it looking so twizzled and frizzed. Draped over her shoulders was a plumeria lei—clearly plastic, as none of the petals even whispered at wilting. At one point in the video, the white man yanked her by that lei, snapped her head back then sucked on the knobby protrusion of her collarbone, mashing a handful of flowers in his fist.

Rather than calling Patti immediately, Mehana scoured the internet for days, trying to understand what her old friend had done and why. Eventually she stumbled upon an online forum into which past and present employees of Get Wild Productions pitched their darkest revelations. A behind-the-scenes look into the infamous Get Wild Productions, into Landon Wilder. Mehana had already researched Get Wild extensively. She knew it'd begun as a kernel of an idea: Hawai'i was a paradise few mainlanders could afford; why not create a virtual, erotic replica featuring the island's most elegant, ethnic beauties? Porn, but make it tropical (with a subscription fee). She knew when it finally launched, sales exceeded expectations. Against her good sense, she pictured sweaty white men from the Midwest clicking their computer mice to the fantasy of fucking a local girl in positions of their choosing. In her mind she watched them writhe and absorbed their moans, while all the users glimpsed of the male actor was the shaft of his penis.

It was only through the forum that Mehana learned of the "confidential" stipulation: that every office employee who self-identified as female—whether it be kānaka maoli Patti as marketing executive or that redheaded receptionist—was contracted to participate in an Island Girl film at least once. Some women waited until the last day of their employment tenure; others got it out of the way during orientation. Regardless, all the women carried with them the same burdensome prerequisite during their time at Get Wild Productions, though Mehana didn't know of this contractual obligation when she first saw her friend on film. She just assumed Patti enjoyed playing culturally insensitive dress-up while getting her ass fucked.

Seeing her old friend splayed out naked on-screen opened a wide crevice inside her. She'd considered the reflection of her own body and all the places where it'd failed her—jellied inner thighs, bulbous neck, the arena of fat around her waist she'd never managed to tone, no matter how many "100 Days, 100 Sit-ups" campaigns she engaged in. It was a terrible exercise, to pare herself open in such a vulnerable way. Terrible until you flipped it on its side, and then it became thrilling.

Mehana had slammed her computer lid shut. She took several deep breaths and tried not to take the affront to heart. This fetishization of local women was nothing new. Landon Wilder was simply the first man in her vicinity to profit from it, a pinch of which also transferred to her old friend Patti. And shouldn't she be happy for Patti? Was this not some sort of reckoning, a taking back of what is ours? She tried to be happy for Patti, but she couldn't get that stupid screenshot of the coconut bra and plastic lei out of her head.

And it wasn't just the props. It was the distillation of everything she'd learned about her Hawaiian self into her friend's naked body. It was watching that naked body pared open for men whose skin gleamed, who probably were making four times as much as her.

It was despising Landon Wilder and wishing to see him suffer.

Or else it was loneliness. For she was so lonely, it spread to her chest and her head and her naʻau, as warm and beaten as a bruised plum, or the gleaming wet of coconut meat.

IN THE MAIN office, there were posters everywhere. Lining the walls and filling space between the clerestory windows and even papering the floor as artwork meant to be trampled. The posters depicted Island Girls in a variety of outfits (coconut bra and lei; aloha shirt unbuttoned to a cavern of cleavage; muʻumuʻu severed above the knees; pareo wrapped discomfitingly around the breasts) and poses (chest out; ass protruding; arms grazing the bellies of other women; toned stomachs pinched up toward the sky), and each one was framed in a matte-black mounting that depressed Mehana, reminding her of funerals and decay.

What else it reminded her of: an interview with Landon Wilder that aired on PBS Hawaii about a month before that Mehana couldn't unremember. It made her thoughts feel hard and fudgy, and as a remedy, she'd made a habit of viewing the broadcast every evening with her fingers roving around inside her underwear, letting his voice barrel through her ligaments and joints, lulling her into an attempt toward pleasure and then to sleep.

His teeth weren't as bad in the interview. She barely noticed the midline diastema.

Landon Wilder and the interviewer leaned on opposite ends of a vinyl-topped cocktail table carved like a lima bean. They sipped from copper-ringed coffee mugs; an elaborate birds-of-paradise floral arrangement split the table in an even half. The old white interviewer nodded his head solemnly as Landon Wilder spoke of bolstering the local economy while ensuring each Island Girl is treated like a Hawaiian princess.

"And how much do you pay these girls?" asked the interviewer.

"I'm not at liberty to disclose that information. Just know our Island Girls are compensated fairly and generously. They are the heart of our enterprise, and without them, Get Wild Productions would not be sustainable and therefore would not be able to give back to the local community as we have done since our inception."

"Do you see your work as diminishing or debasing to Hawaiian culture?"

"Well, Craig, I'd love to turn that question back onto you. You're Irish, no? Do you find St. Patrick's Day celebrations diminishing or debasing? The local ones, now, like at Murphy's, where they raise much-needed funds for Kapi'olani Children's Hospital. Does this bastardizing of a cultural holiday offend you personally?"

"I don't believe so, no."

"And why do you think that is?"

"Well, I'd say knowing we're all coming together to raise money for the keiki makes me feel the celebration has a higher purpose than just dressing up as leprechauns and drunks."

"That's exactly it, then, isn't it? We, too, at Get Wild Productions are working toward a higher purpose—that purpose being to revive the local economy. Did you know, every other fiscal year, we donate fifteen percent of our profits to island-based organizations? Call up the Hawaii Foodbank, the Nature Conservancy, Hawaii Land Trust, even the Audubon Society, and ask how they've benefited as mission partners of Get Wild Productions. Each and every one of our local partners has nothing but good things to say about us."

"And remind me, how much of those profits goes to the talent?"

"Again, I'm not at liberty to say."

Now in the main office, Landon Wilder walked with confidence and speed, and Mehana struggled to maintain pace.

"Our Island Girls get final say on all marketing materials that feature their talent, including video advertisements," he explained as they moved through a labyrinth of cubicles and freestanding desks. "We've also established a specific algorithm to gift our talent a portion of the profits we make for every video view over a thirty-day period. We call it a bang bonus, get it?"

"Ha-ha." Mehana wrapped the purse strap around her chest. She imagined chucking a wad of spittle in his face.

They passed through the marketing department quickly, too quick to look for Patti, though Mehana assumed she was there, adrift in a current of cubicles, polishing contracts or filing her nails. Honestly she didn't really know what Patti's job entailed. For all she knew, Patti was holed up in the dressing room, adjusting the twine straps of her coconut bra so as not to leave an imprint on her skin.

But this wasn't about Patti, was it?

Except the moment they pushed through the heavy security door and emerged into the Get Wild Productions film studio, Mehana fingered her purse strap then asked Landon if he knew a Patti Tanabe. And Landon Wilder looked down on her like she'd just asked to see his cock.

"Patti, sure. Marketing, right? Patti's great."

"She sent me the audition listing. We went to high school together, but we sorta lost touch after that. She stayed here to get her MBA at UH, and I went to the East Coast. I think we were always a bit jealous of each other . . ."

Her voice trailed off. Landon Wilder was smiling in a way that sent chicken skin currenting over her arms and legs.

"You're quirky. I enjoy that in my Girls."

"Thank you." It sounded like *fuck you* in her mouth.

The studio lights pulsed around them, suffusing the room in so much heat, Mehana felt sweat building up between her thighs. The studio resembled a newsroom, what with its teleprompters and high beams, a professional green screen draped over the back wall. Yet there was also the considerately determined furnishings: contemporary sectional, stern oak end tables, a king mattress draped in an oleander Hawaiian quilt.

Her heels adhered to the vinyl floors.

Landon Wilder was looking at her funny.

"Look, I don't normally do this without a full audition, but I've got a pretty good gut sense, and right now it's telling me to take a chance on you. Hell, you're friends with Patti, you're already part of the Get Wild 'ohana!"

A hand descended on her shoulder. Fingers grazed her collarbone like the blades of a paper fan.

"The role's yours if you want it. Though we'll need to do something about that skin . . ."

WHAT THEY DID was they sprayed her with a shade of dihydroxyacetone perfectly calibrated to her body chemistry. They toweled her off and exfoliated dead skin from her pelvis and from the soles of her feet. They didn't dare wax her now, in case she suffered from sensitive skin prone to irritation, so instead a grandmotherly aesthetician tweezed hair after hair from the trenches of her pubic line.

"Tweezing ain't ideal. Sorry, honey," the aesthetician offered.

Mehana dug tiny parentheses into the soft pads of her palms and tried to smile.

After, the aesthetician left her alone in a tiled room where she was meant to sample several Island Girl costumes and choose one to her liking. The fact that she was afforded a choice at all seemed insane to her. She rifled through a purse that no longer felt like hers and opened her phone to four emails and two voicemails from Gina. Depressingly, none were all that urgent. Only in the second voicemail did Gina mention Mehana's absence, while the emails were all forwarded signed contracts for Mehana to file accordingly. She scanned the names now: Heather Wilkinson, Gracie Thomas, Genevieve Hunt, Caroline Jones. White woman names. She made sure to archive one of the emails so that her inbox only contained three (lest her mother's superstition about the number four prove true). She tossed her phone to the bottom of her purse, where it sunk like a cinder brick.

She tried on the costumes. A full-length mirror lined the makai wall, and Mehana stripped off her paisley blouse and slacks under the popcorn ceiling, unhooked her black bralette lined by delicate lace. She examined her body in just its black underwear and heels. She kicked the heels off. She had a trim waist, but poor eating habits had ringed her belly in that circle of fat. Her forearms were lithe but her biceps droopy; her thighs quivery and immense. She didn't like her posture, the way her shoulders caved in and inflated the already paunchy tissue of her arms. She tried standing straighter, her neck erect, her chin protruding like a nēnē goose. She imagined this stance before a green screen. There, better.

Get Wild Productions had branded each costume with a name tag. She tried the first her hands had located, clenching the rounded tip of the hanger and folding open the tag: *Island Girl, Hula Edition*. Draped over the hanger was a pleated grass skirt stitched together by waxy artificial fringe and a coconut bra resembling what Patti had sported in her audition tape years prior. Mehana snorted. What did she expect? Kukui-stained pāʻū, vibrant crimson kūpeʻe to hook round her ankles and wrists, lei ʻāʻī to drape her shoulders, lei poʻo to crown her head? Please. Mehana tugged the grass skirt up her thighs, then teased the elastic band to accommodate her rounds of fat. She folded the coconut bra over her chest and cinched it tight by double-knotting the green twine just below her breasts then bringing the hollowed coconut shells forward. At least her breasts remembered how to be twentysomething.

The getup reminded her of a role-play costume Karl had bought her last month in an innocuous attempt to enhance their sex life. The tag: *Enjoy that first day of school feeling with our Sexy Prep School Girl!* It was about two sizes too small, and the plaid trim on the blouse sleeves tickled her arms like mad. Still, she rallied. Pinned two plaid bows into her tresses and wore the glasses and the button-down skirt, even though she couldn't get all the buttons clasped, and the bridge of the glasses kept slipping down her nose. She knew Karl came from the exultant quiver of his lower lip, just as she knew she did not from simply being too close to her own body. Karl, inherently awkward, didn't know how to talk about the costume afterward without his neck bursting into hives. It was the most daring feat in the history of their sex life, and they never did it again.

A knock on the door sideswept her thoughts. Mehana turned the brass knob to find Patti waiting there with her arms crossed. Her lips were a flat red line; her eyes swam glassy and dead.

"Rhona said I'd find you here." She scanned Mehana from toes to tops, then snorted. "Nice outfit. Looks familiar."

"I'm choosing a different one," Mehana said hurriedly.

But Patti waved her off while inserting a new, charged air into the room. "Don't worry about it, only teasing. You look good. But jeez, what did she do to your skin?"

Mehana lifted a forearm perforce. "That bad?"

"You look like . . . a pumpkin."

Patti straddled the crooked arm of the suede loveseat. She sat there so crudely, Mehana couldn't get out of her head the image of Landon Wilder slotted under her; his thighs fanned out, his cock meaty and erect.

"I'll be honest, I'm surprised you showed. You seemed to hold very strong opinions about Landon just a few hours ago."

Mehana felt her left breast sag under the coconut shell.

"I don't feel differently," she said. "Just need the money, you know that."

Patti nodded thoughtfully. "I respect that. Just some quick advice, then, before you head in. Landon fucks the new girls at least once, preferably on camera. He fucks them in the ass as part of the audition, and then he makes you sign a contract. He'll convince you to stay on with Get Wild as an actress, even if you don't want to. He's charming like that." She paused to examine her cuticles. "I know you think you're better than me; you have since high school. Thing is, though, you became an Island Girl the moment you strung up that coconut bra. Might as well enjoy the sex. Landon's got himself a diamond of a dick."

She closed the door, and Mehana pressed her ear to the *ker-clack, ker-clack* of Patti's stiletto heels prancing back to marketing. She stared at the suede loveseat, where Patti's ass had left a deep burgundy pattern like when a vacuum redirects the fibers of a carpet. It was an artful stain, one Mehana hoped to re-create. She positioned her pelvis in a reenactment of Patti's posture. She straddled the armrests until the friction of her underwear against her clit pullulated a precise pleasure from between her legs, a fist reaching through ocean muck to pull back a pearl. She proceeded in this manner until a knock kicked her out of her own head, out of her body, and Rhona the receptionist peered in and issued a countdown: five minutes till call time.

She adjusted her coconut bra for the last time then left the room.

MEHANA HAD BEEN thinking for some time that if Karl asked her to marry him, she would say yes. She thought about quitting Gina's without giving proper notice, and she considered the audacity of shutting off all the reception room lights then taking a few hundred contracts with her. She wouldn't start her own talent agency; no, Mehana was nowhere near that assured in her own competence. She just liked the idea of leaving Gina head-scratchingly puzzled in the dark.

She liked the idea of resuming a friendship with Patti, however strained and in sore need of maintenance. Despite what Patti had said, Mehana had never thought herself better than her, though clearly Patti had woven through a series of escalating poor choices that'd ultimately wedged her somewhere between Landon Wilder's cock and heart, rendering her indispensable to his enterprise. She didn't want to learn Landon and Patti were in love. Didn't want to think about his balls bashing into anyone's fleshy ass but hers.

She thought about the rabbit head vibrator, this new and invaluable purchase, bringing her one day to orgasm.

She thought especially of this elusive orgasm as she reclined on the staged bed, the mattress surprisingly and unpleasantly firm under her pelvis, her lower belly bared raw and tentacled by stretchmarks. She would do anything to airbrush them from the film, and to maintain the illusion that Patti had so carefully constructed of skin pulled healthy and taut, as if this was how a woman's tissue was meant to feel. She sighed. Her poor parents, though thank god they'd gone primitive and hocked their technology the day Trump was inaugurated. Still, word got around. Folks talked. But she couldn't think about that now. She drew a long breath and reminded her head and her cunt: they were about to fuck Landon Wilder. For how much money, Mehana hadn't asked. Why the fuck hadn't she asked? She spread her legs and waited for further instruction.

"We don't like giving our Island Girls a script," Landon had explained before the aesthetician had taken her away. "Our viewers appreciate that sort of authentic, amateur vibe that comes with not quite knowing what comes next in the role play. That way, none of our Girls ever have to fake their surprise."

He'd asked if she was open to this risk of the unexpected, and of course she'd said yes. For the past five years, she'd stretched out her arms to welcome the risk of the unexpected, only to be beaten back by gales both traditional and sad. Now, here she was, an Island Girl in training. It was the most unexpected thing that had happened to her, and still she could see this fate tunneling toward her from a mile away.

Lying belly-up, Mehana grew increasingly insensate, so much so she nearly missed the rapacious blaring of an alarm. Sheaves of sound cloistered the studio, metrical at first, before mutating into something dark and discordant. A door opened, swung shut. The overhead lights burst like the birth of small galaxies. A woman tugged on Mehana's arm with an alarming insouciance, brought her up and standing so fast she felt her brain scramble and the blood in her body plunge skyward.

Above the studio doors, a red strobe light whirled patterns across the ceiling.

A fire drill, then. But was there time to change into a proper outfit?

Then bodies were brushing up against her, bodies both wraithlike and gamine, dressed in far more layers than Mehana was and speaking in frenetic tones.

"But it's just a drill," said Mehana.

No one corrected her, so when she first smelled the smoke, Mehana figured it was some microwaved-lunch disaster that'd occurred simultaneously with the fire drill. Building maintenance scheduled routine drills all the time. There was one season at Gina's when fire drills took place three times a week, at precisely the same hour. She learned to avoid reheating her coffee for a good ten minutes before two, when the alarm would undoubtedly resound through the building's twelve floors and send its occupants fleeing. What a curious role play, she'd think, scurrying down the stairwell in a false display of dramaturgy.

Now, dressed in the actual costume of role play, Mehana found herself desensitized to the scurry and the taking shelter, to the echoing clatter of several thousand heels clacking down forty flights of stairs. The smoke built, seeping through cracks in the doors and tumbling down the stairs. She brought her hands to her bare body. Her clutch of belly bounced beneath the coconut shells. She tried very hard to pay no mind to the classily clad women passing judgment on her outfit, her turgid, untoned tissue. The smoke wove through the byways of her nasal cavity. By the tenth floor, descending hurriedly onto the ninth story landing, Mehana realized she might die there, among all those high heels, painstakingly naked in her culture's most devastating clichés. She would die as one of Landon Wilder's Island Girls. She would die sans orgasm, sans friends. Really she couldn't think of a more fitting end to a brief and adequate life than to die of smoke inhalation in the Executive Center stairwell.

Mehana emerged on the ground floor. She was still wearing the coconut bra and waxy plastic grass skirt and her feet were bare. She was alive. Cars scraped by along Bishop Street, their drivers hooting at her, jeering. She brought her arms to her chest. A hand flattened over her shoulder. It was Patti, offering her a flannel cover-up.

She hurried with the flannel, bringing her arms through the sleeves, drawing the collar flaps tight around her neck. Patti flashed her a featureless grin, leaving her hand to rest on Mehana's shoulder.

"To be honest, you pull off that look much better than I do."

"Please. I can already feel this stupid tan running."

Patti glanced up at the twinkling glass tower, peering around for smoke. Mehana followed suit.

"Think we'll finally watch it all burn down?" Mehana asked.

Patti shook her head sadly. "Nah, these white dudes will outlive us all. Might as well wring out some pleasure for ourselves while we still can, right?"

Pleasure piled like a stack of stones in her chest, then, leaning into the delicious pressure of Patti's palm. So she was forgiven, at least temporarily. Patti still grinning noncommittally, fire truck sirens trumpeting in the distance. Mehana adjusted her drooping coconut bra from inside the tent of flannel. Landon Wilder was nowhere to be seen.

"We should have dinner," Mehana proposed.

"Tonight?"

"Can't. I think I have a date with Karl. I should probably check. What is today?"

Patti peered at her phone. "Wednesday."

"Wednesday," Mehana said, testing the syllables on her tongue. "Yes, I think we've planned to date tonight. Tomorrow?"

"Kevin and I are seeing *Les Misérables*. Diamond Head Theatre's putting it on."

"Sometime soon, then?"

Patti's smile flattened like an upturned blade. "Yes, absolutely."

She squeezed Mehana's shoulder, and then she was gone.

Mehana stood still on the shit-splotched sidewalk, waiting for someone to shove her off her axis, or maybe to reassure her everything will be fine. She will orgasm one day, and she won't lose her job. Gina will understand; likely she will promote her. Karl will fulfill her complicated needs. She and Patti will reconnect over an extravagant meal, someplace sun-kissed and inauthentically red-bricked, like Livestock Tavern or Fête, where she can return the flannel Patti had so kindly loaned her. Over a tray of chilled oysters, the women will forgive each other slowly, and Mehana will think with enormous confidence, *I am growing*.

Eventually, building management waves everyone inside.

Patti's flannel is taken from her, the crimps in her grass skirt smoothed by a handheld iron, her hair brushed back by boar bristles. What a strange new way to live that she has mined. Cameras whirl around her, striking high beams blink on and off and on again, and then Landon Wilder is stepping into a puddle of light, his naked body whitewashed and glossy under the fluorescents. Mehana lies supine on the mattress, sneaking glimpses of his bullet chest and stiff, knuckled belly, and legs hilariously skinny as chopsticks. She tries exceedingly hard not to laugh. Something new sounds out from between her thighs; it resembles the sound of her own unmaking. This whole Island Girls thing is tricky business indeed, though Mehana thinks she is getting the hang of it.

God, her poor ancestors. This grass skirt and fake coconut bra. How would they feel?

But no time to think of that now. Now, legs splayed out like the tallowy ends of a candle, Mehana holds tight to the feeling that anything is possible. It is possible to be many things, all the time, all at once.

The Love and Decline of the Corpse Flower

I sneeze into the corpse flower and a geyser of spittle settles over the leaves. Who buys a corpse flower for a dead woman's wake? In the wake of your wife's death, here is a plant of intolerable fragrance. No friend of mine, I decide, shearing a pinch of the sealed maroon spathe between my fingers, surrendering it to my dead wife's listing floors.

With no one left occupying the house, I pluck the enormous potted plant from the lip of the marble counter to send it elsewhere. The bathroom, perhaps. Or maybe the yard. Weeds sprouting like pinpricks knitting through the parched grass. Haunani was meticulous in the keeping of that yard, so it's nice to see the plot go to shit now. Like finally we have carved out some breathing room.

The pot sinks like a weighted blanket in my hands, its awful column stretching nearly three feet tall, and it's true I don't want this stupid plant anywhere near this house, but what about ghosts? What of returning spirits and lingering losses, of adhering to your wife's last wishes that her home be infested by the raging flora of her friends? I drop the plant on the couch, give it Haunani's favorite reclining spot on the narrow chaise longue. Can't risk more curses, not in this home. Already I'm sneezing, drooling like a dog who's fractured a tooth, so you better believe I'm not messing around. Just think the plant looks perfectly fine on the chaise longue. Sits up alert, like Haunani in her living years. I'm almost tempted to drape it with a sheet.

The rest of the house is budding chaos and can rightly stay that way. Folks are gone, day's pau, I'm a widow in no rush. I check that the curtains are drawn, and then I'm loosening my slate-black wrap dress, letting it fall to the floor like sloughed skin. Underneath I'm wearing bulky cotton underwear, no bra. My thick neck choked by a string of Tahitian pearls. My hair tumbles in gray ribbons. An old, fat widow. Finally.

I recline on the sofa with a tumbler of gin and a bag of dried li hing mui, the powder so sour it makes my tongue pucker. It's like sucking on a lemon rind. I eat the plums slowly and consider what to do with all these potted plants. A chaos of competing floral fragrances ripples through the rooms, and with each new breath I fight the wash of hibiscus, snowy gardenias, pīkake, yellow 'ilima in full bloom. Anela will be here soon to help me with this mess. She will know exactly where to situate these flowers to keep me from going crazy as I live out the rest of my days in this house.

Anela is teaching me about curses and last wishes. She and I were mostly quilting-class acquaintances until her husband keeled over from a heart attack and a particularly trying bout of pneumonia rushed Haunani to the hospital, and then we found ourselves idling in a sterile waiting room, counting the green swirls marbling the beige walls while we waited for news. In regard to her impending loss, Anela was impossibly frank. Said we were too old to bother with playing obtuse, and then a surgeon emerged through the wings of the ICU to tell her her husband didn't make it. Since that day we have been dear friends.

It wasn't until recently in our friendship I learned of her peculiar affinity for curses. Now she is the beacon to guide my voyage into widowdom. Widowhood? Both sound frightfully eclectic. I'm lucky to have her, because really I don't know what to do with all these plants, the corpse flower especially. Doesn't a significant allergic reaction, its inordinate size, and repulsive smell warrant reconsideration of a dead wife's last wish?

Last time Anela was here, she pointed at a scuff mark on the wall, an indentation cupped like an apostrophe. She scrunched her nose like she was smelling something rancid and declared the house haunted. A routine haunting, she said. Nothing to fret over, but I should be careful not to disturb the spirits in the walls any further. Haunani was in hospice at the time, declining in the bedroom upstairs, talking to her pīkake plant. I watched Anela analyze the scuff mark. I felt the walls shiver around me.

Supposedly, the house was haunted when Haunani first bought it, but this wasn't something we talked about. I was distracted by its place on the Hawai'i Register of Historic Places, and Haunani was preoccupied by my unfamiliar presence in her home. Middle-aged and newly migratory, we skated around each other, the chaos of every closed cabinet, every clatter of silverware amplified, our lovemaking fierce and tender. At night, I watched finger-sized cockroaches scuttle across the ceiling. Fell asleep to the chirp of geckos, the echo flushing over the walls. Haunani's hand over my breast like an opened jaw. I felt hands all around me, prying things open, battering others shut. During the day Haunani filled the house with florals, and this, too, was new to me. She took pride in her hobbyist botany, her inherited green thumb. She loved her indoor anthuriums, tended to her outdoor pōhinahina shrubs with the meticulous care one affords her own child. I grew up differently. Before Haunani, all my plants either died or lived under the waxy gloss of plastic.

Now I wonder how the spirits in the walls can manage living among all these smells.

Then the doorbell rings. I retire the gin and the li hing mui to the wrapped rattan coffee table. As I weave the black dress back around my body, I try very hard not to look at the corpse flower, lithe and erect on the chaise longue. I drape a blanket over it.

"THAT'S A PECULIAR choice," Anela says. As with all today's visitors, Anela brings with her a potted plant, a quiet blooming anthurium with waxy red spathes peeling open like a woman's heart. There the anthurium goes, beside the swaddled corpse flower.

"I didn't know what else to do with it. Look at the thing, it's monstrous."

"It's a corpse flower, that's sort of the point." Anela helps herself to the glass of gin, takes a dainty sip then jostles backward like I've shot her. "Gross. Gin and li hing? Another peculiar choice."

Anela sits beside the potted anthurium. Her cheeks are brushed with too much powder again, her gray hair permed in tight springs. She looks to be around 190 years old, though in reality she's probably in her seventies, like me.

"I haven't seen one of those in ages," she says. "Who brought you a corpse flower?"

"I'm not sure. Janet, I think? Or maybe it was Nalani. Or Trisha, she's always hated me. I should've kept a list. I should've written all this down. How am I supposed to write thank-you notes?"

I should call my son, I think. How nice to believe him the one who sent this flower, for at least this would mean he's thinking of his mother.

I sit beside Anela on what's left of the couch cushion, hide my face in the sag of her breasts.

"Oh, darling, don't you worry. No one expects much from you, you're grieving. Come on now, we've work to do."

We spend the rest of the evening walking in and out of rooms, bumping into furniture, redecorating. Always pots are in our hands. I wedge the hibiscus behind the toilet, store the lokelani rose on the refrigerator. Anela arranges the blooming 'ilima on the bottom shelf of a bookcase. She says to pay attention to the way the light folds over a flower's stem, its tender wet petals. I try to shove the corpse flower in the closet, but the rising spadix snags on the doorframe, and when I lean into the plant, its foul smell sends me backward, grasping for the bed frame.

"Anela, you need to smell this thing. I *cannot* have it in my house!"

Anela climbs the stairs slowly, brings her full face to its newly budding spathes. "And that, doll, is how the corpse flower got its name. Best to leave it in the living room, then."

"You can't be serious."

"Granted it's not the prettiest flower, but you surely don't want this thing in your bedroom when it starts to bloom. You'll be smelling rotting flesh for days, weeks maybe. Best to keep it near the kitchen, where it can fight with the smells of your awful home cooking."

"Anela, I am *not* keeping this in my house. I can't live with this thing! It's going to make the whole place smell like death!"

But Anela is too busy squatting at the knees, lifting the pot by its pliable rim. "You say that as if you have a choice," she says. "Now lift with your knees, not your back!"

We move the plant together, back to the chaise longue.

AFTER FINDING HOMES for each of the plants, I treat Anela to a buffet spread of leftovers from the wake, and I don't ask her why she didn't come. We eat straight from the containers because neither of us can be bothered to wash dishes. She's brought a dime bag and rolling paper with her, and while she packs a joint between her shriveled fingers, I dip my head into the corpse flowerpot, holding my breath. Someone is mowing the yard across the street, a blistering labor sound, and a dog barks.

Anela is talking about the food brought to grieving widows. How when her husband died, most of the deliveries were variations of the same chicken, rice, and cheese casserole. How I should be grateful for this rosemary risotto, or is it orzo? I chew on a spear of particularly tough chicken and watch the warm light of the lamp bend around the flower's jutting column. Really it's a phallic shape that has no place in this house, but I throw another blanket on it anyway. Prop up the pillow that sags beneath the pot's weight. I think again about calling my son—an ornithologist, but still in the realm of biology, no?—but this would require a significant level of intoxication, and Anela is in no hurry with her joint.

"Maybe we could call the museum," I say. "They might take the plant. It's a marvel of nature's engineering."

That something quite this grotesque can go on living.

"I don't think the museum wants your flower, and anyway we can't move it from the house. You'll disturb the spirits, and Haunani will have no chance of being at peace. You need to do this the right way."

"I'm so tired," I say.

"I know, honey," she says. "Got a light?"

I pass her a lighter. She takes a long time rotating the joint, blooming a soft cherry. A few hits, and she ashes the joint before handing it to me. I do the same.

"I feel like I should be crying or something," I say.

"You will eventually, don't you worry about that."

"But I can't bother with anything but these stupid flowers now. Now I'm the crazy flower lady with hundreds of plants, and by the time I finish watering them all, I'll just have to start all over again."

Anela reclines beside me. "Yes, plants are old-fashioned that way. Very needy little things."

"I have better things to do with my retirement."

Over forty-five years of driving the same bus route for a rotating parcel of grade-school keiki and I actually can't think of anything better to do with my retirement than garden. Next week, perhaps I will visit the aquarium. See the world's largest clam, a fleshy bivalve, and a sea of striped manini. I will pay kama'āina entrance to the Honolulu Zoo and feed the goats. It's something I'd once hoped to do with my own grandchildren, but now I can't even see my son loaning me his child long enough for a shift in the petting zoo.

"You should come back to quilting class," Anela says. "Cathy is teaching the naupaka pattern next week. You could complete your collection!"

"I think I'll call my son tomorrow," I say. "He might know how to care for these plants. He could help me. Tell me what to do with the corpse flower, at least."

She ashes the joint then works to reignite the cherry, twirls the paper like a circus baton. "I already told you what to do with the corpse flower. The minute you move it, the house's spirits will throw a fit. And Haunani's spirit will be lost at sea. Is that what you want?"

"Yes, that's what I want," I say.

She hands me the casserole. "Eat some more. You are *so* cranky."

I sneeze into the corpse flower. "I think I'm allergic to this one."

But of course she doesn't believe me.

I THINK THE reason Anela did not come to the wake is because she's uncomfortable around death. It's the same reason why, when the surgeon ushered her into a private room to deliver the news about her husband, she brought me with her. "This is my sister," she lied, and when the man ventured around the word *dead*, citing "best efforts" and "too much damage done," she spoke very slowly. "You are not a ballerina, you don't have to tiptoe. Tell me exactly what happened to my husband."

We went out for drinks after that. Got so drunk we couldn't remember where the hospital was, how we'd gotten to the downtown bar in the first place. Haunani was still admitted, pneumonia crippling her already weakened limbs. At some point Anela went home, and I found my way back to the fourth floor, where my wife had reclined the hospital bed all the way flat, her breathing regulated by the chemical hum of machines, a television screening nonsense against the wall. She was asleep. I felt guilty for leaving. I went down to the gift shop and bought her an enormous bouquet with all the cash I had left in my wallet. An artfully woven bundle of anthuriums, birds-of-paradise, white orchids in full bloom, a collection of red ginger. Something the tag called "tropical foliage." I positioned the bouquet on her tray table, where a plate of chicken slathered in a gelatinous gravy lay untouched.

It wasn't Haunani's first or last hospitalization, but it was the one I'll remember with a frightening clarity, and I'm scared it has nothing to do with her and everything to do with Anela.

I can understand avoiding the funeral, the awful archaic burial underground, but why bother evading a wake? If anything it's more party than grievous affair, and Anela loves her parties.

Here's something else about Anela: she and Haunani go way back. Further than our time in quilting class, further still than my time with Haunani. While I was busy acclimating to a husband and a young son, Anela and Haunani flourished as daughters of the sixties, casting spells on ʻōhiʻa stamens, conducting elaborate prayer rituals tucked in the Koʻolau mountains. Braiding each other's hair. They spent months, years, rotating in and out of the same karaoke bars, a cycle of friendly māhūs buying them drinks and calling them *nani, nani*. This, of course, was all relayed to me by Anela, and to this day I don't know much about the bounds of this friendship, when or why it hurtled to its eventual end.

Anela was the first person I told about Haunani's last wish to see her home sowed new with flowers, potted plants. She said, "That sounds like Haunani," but how could she be so sure?

I suppose all this is buried now, and here are these plants in my dead wife's house. My house, where I'm meant to eat and sleep and shit. Where I never bothered with the frivolities of interior design because I hadn't ever the time, or the drive, or maybe because it would always be Haunani's name on the house and I would always be the one who moved in guiltily after leaving my own family behind.

I REALLY DO it, the next day. I pick up the phone and call my son. Lono doesn't answer. I walk around the kitchen pressing my hand against all the surfaces: stiff, wet, leathery, chilled. I open the fridge but there are only wrinkled tangerines and a carton of expired skim milk. Before I can scribble a grocery list, my phone rings.

"I thought you might be interested that I recently acquired a corpse flower," I say. Wander the kitchen in nondescript circles because this is the only way I know how to talk on a cell phone.

"Congratulations," Lono says. My son, how he has grown into his voice! The thrumming bass reverberates over miles and miles of invisible power lines that have woven together to create this exchange. A slurry of errant voices strains over the call. I imagine Lono adrift among the chaos of a vibrant research lab, his cubicle littered with scientific discoveries, family photos. Perhaps I am in one of those photos, though maybe this is too strong of a wish.

Only since Haunani got sick did Lono start taking my calls at all, which made me think ill of him.

"Have you ever seen a corpse flower?" I ask. "The thing really does smell like a corpse!"

"Guess that's how it got its name. Hey, do you need something? I'm a little busy here."

Of course. Very busy, my little ornithologist.

"I was wondering if you would like to come over and see the flower. I suspect it's not going to last very long, and I'm actually working to get rid of it soon. A scientist like yourself might be interested—"

"I'm not a botanist," he says.

"I know that. But plants, birds, they all exist on this earth, do they not?"

His sigh is clipped. "Look, I've got more important things to do than visit with you and see your plant. I really don't care about plants. I definitely don't want to be in that house. I'm sure you can understand that."

A soft clicking emanates from the walls. Ghosts, I suspect. But now is not the time for this intrusion.

"I understand," I say. "I'm doing fine, by the way. Haunani is dead and the house is haunted and I haven't a clue what to do with all these plants, but I'm fine. I have Anela. I have my new indoor garden. The house is haunted. I hear the walls talking to me now—"

But Lono has already hung up the phone.

I press my ear to the wall. Fold my fingers over the sunken indentation, I sniff the scuff mark and pretend

I'm Anela. But it just smells like old paint. The walls stop clicking, and the silence is louder than anything I've ever heard.

THE ONLY WAY to stop feeling so awful is to take a nap. When I wake up, I'm lying crooked on the sofa, and the corpse flower is staring down at me just as it was when I first fell asleep, except now something is different. The corpse flower has an arm.

A full arm, to be precise, which means there is a hand affixed to the end of it, five fingers that beetle forward from a shriveled palm. Five nails bitten to shorn nubs, bruised by the burden of decay. The arm, too, is pasty, snatched of veins, so cold. Dead.

I reach out to touch the arm, startling it. It recoils. Not dead. It disappears behind the frill of red spathe, folded open like a pleated skirt. "Is someone there?" I ask. The plant stills, forlorn. Perhaps the arm is gone for good. Is it possible that the flower's glorious spire now sags ever so slightly? Plants, according to Anela, are far more fickle than humans. Supposedly, plants teach us patience, but I've had enough practice. Driving a school bus and being many wives. I do not need a corpse flower to teach me.

"If this is some queer garden trick, I'm not interested," I say.

The corpse flower doesn't respond. I back into the wall, where a few dozen little apostrophes now litter the clapboard. My god, they are multiplying! My stomach lurches. Last I ate was the casserole with Anela and two lonely hits off her joint. I remove some meat-and-cheese phenomenon from the fridge and gouge at it cold with a clean spoon. The sensation is one of combing through wet soil, but at least I'm no longer hungry. When I return to the wall, the marks are still there. I sit beside the corpse flower, wondering what to do with all my time.

"You might be hallucinating," Anela says over the phone, after I've told her about the arm. "I've heard sometimes the terrible smell can do things to a person."

So much time I didn't welcome, because the truth is, I didn't so much retire from driving the school bus as I did accept a lovely little severance package following a particularly unfortunate incident with a spoiled third grader, a pocketknife, and a field-trip ruckus I found distracting and hazardous to my job at hand. I didn't stop the bus. Got the kids back to campus safely and the pocketknife's victim only required two stitches! Two. Do two stitches even necessitate a hospital visit? Yes.

When I lost my job, I told Anela before I told Haunani. I'd like to say this was because of my wife's ill health at the time. That I was shielding her from further hardship.

"I called Lono this morning," I say. "But before the whole arm incident, so I couldn't tell him about it."

"Gracious, honey, I'm *glad* you didn't tell him! He already thinks you're nutty. I can't believe you called him."

I clench the phone harder, dismayed. Why shouldn't a mother call her son? Just because she's left his father to remarry—and this time for love! I carried him. I *birthed* him.

"He was happy to hear from me," I say. The words flashy and inflated, like an old Elvis tune that thrums nostalgic against my tongue. "He says I should call more often. He might even stop by soon to see the corpse flower."

Anela asks if I'm eating, if I'm sleeping enough. She speaks as though we didn't just share a joint yesterday. She asks how the plants are doing.

"Other than the arm in the corpse flower, they're doing just fine."

Over the past day and a half, I've watched the ginger keel over, the plumeria cluster melt under the onslaught of sun. My poor lokelani rose plant wilted overnight. The hibiscus spent a few hours wedged behind the toilet before giving in to nature's cyclical destruction. I flushed the toilet and saw ruby petals swept over the floors like spirals of sand. There is no one left in this house to blame other than the invisible, wall-churning spirits, except I'm the one not watering the plants. Only the corpse flower seems to flourish.

"If you're really seeing an arm," she says slowly. "Then perhaps it's time to get your eyes checked."

But by the time I hang up the phone, the arm has returned, overhanging the sofa pillow like a construction crane. Along with the arm, there is now a sensationally slender thigh, one dressed in age spots and clawing varicose veins that taper down to the petite pleasure of a foot pocked with gemstones. Five toes, a recent pedicure. The arm and the leg are positioned on opposite ends of the corpse flower so as to curate an illusion of balance. I sit down beside it.

"Can you hear me?" I ask. The plant doesn't move. I survey the arm, the leg, all the flowy digits for signs of a spirit. I decide to try something new. "If you can hear me, maybe you'll try raising one finger? Or one toe? Though I suspect a finger might be more natural."

The arm raises a finger. Its ring finger, where a band of white cinches around otherwise tanned flesh.

I am thrilled. "Wonderful! All right then, how about what you're doing here. What exactly is it that you want?"

The corpse flower's finger goes quiet. I try again.

"Are you happy here? On the couch, in this house?"

The ring finger lifts again. Hovers over the sofa like a plane fixed in mid-descent.

"Will you stay here for a while?"

Yes.

"Will you grow new appendages?"

Yes.

"Are you trapped in a corpse flower?"

Yes.

"Can I help you?"

No.

★ ★ ★

HAUNANI STILL DEAD, summer turning over on its side like a creature roused from slumber. I've resolved to reenter the world in phases.

I rejoin the Wednesday quilting class. Cathy is nearly halfway through the naupaka instruction, but I am a fast learner, my fingers deft and dexterous, and the tūtū are in awe of my quilt's symmetry, the concrete shape my stitches hold. Anela fixes me across the worktable, her fingers folded like little fangs over her quilting needles. She is happy to see me here, but there's something else, too, like she can peer through the curtains of my smile and see all the plants I've watched die over the course of a few weeks. We retire to the balcony after class, sipping iced teas and gumming on scones that crumble in our laps, sharing stories of our families. I listen to the aggrandizement of grandchildren; the prizes they've won, the girls who have their heart. It is impossible to buy into the authenticity of each tale, so of course I take creative liberties myself when sharing news of Lono, his bird research, his subdued yet pleasant wife, his own growing child. I am interested in the visual reactions, how the tūtū glow as if kindled by embers. They ask me if I miss driving the bus, if I had longed to see my grandchild as a passenger before speeding into retirement. I watch the shifting muscles in Anela's face and say yes, yes.

I accept dinner invitations. Couples with hearing aids and metal in their hips, lifelong friends of Haunani's. I dine at a ritzy Kāhala retirement community with Suze, who worked as a music teacher at the elementary school. We nurse ribbons of overcooked pork and speak grandly of the keiki who sunnied our mornings, the parents who looked down on us. A man in a polished vest and bow tie pours us decaf coffee. I ask Suze how much she's spending here, and she says how lucky she is Herb finalized his life insurance policy years ago.

I attend a grief group, just for kicks. But the plastic chairs do a number on my back and everyone in mourning is half my age at least.

I write long emails to my son that I never send.

All the while, I anticipate this great loss either walloping me unexpectedly or abrading my fragile frame over time. To pass through the house and sniff the corpse flower then keel over from all that awful grief. To miss Haunani so bad I consider several ways I might join her. And I do miss her, I miss her.

All the while, the corpse flower blossoms with new limbs. I watch its petaled skirt unfurl over the pot as a new arm, a leg, an elongated neck spring from its vegetative torso. The skin is always rubbery and lacquered in blue veins. When I reach out to make contact, the limb withdraws. The neck is a ghastly, bulbous thing, a buoy that ricochets off the swell of the flower's sprouting spire. I take baby steps, getting to know it. I ask more questions, more lifting of the ring finger. I ask if one day I will hear it talk.

"I would like to stop calling you *it*," I say. "Will you tell me your name?"

No.

"May I guess your name?"

No.

"Do I already know your name?"

Yes.

But the next time Anela pays a visit, the body parts are gone.

Anela scours the house, surveys the grueling state of the wake flowers, clicks her tongue. I trail behind her like a child whose wall drawings have been found out. She asks me how hard is it, how hard is it *really*, to make an effort? I ask why she cares so much, and it is an unkind question—caring is all either of us has left.

"At least this guy is doing well," she says, petting the corpse flower's unwound petals.

"It's a she," I say.

"I apologize, a common mistake. But whew! That *smell*. Honestly I don't know how you live like this."

I sit beside the corpse flower, my knees clenching like cinched knots. Some days I walk perfectly fine, albeit a bit ploddingly, and other days I collapse under the chaos of lashes and spasms, the twinges that current through my body like misfired electricity. I lean against the pot and breathe slowly.

"I'm feeling almost happy about this," I say. "Like all of the other flowers were meant to die so that she could live. I think this is what was always supposed to happen."

"Or you're just dreadfully bad at taking care of plants."

"I suppose it's one or the other."

"Seems like you've managed the whole arm fiasco," she says. "I'll admit you had me more than slightly concerned."

"I am growing," I say. I'm not quite sure what I mean by this, though it rings as something Lono might say. The whole room smells like the curdled remains of a clogged disposal, like a cat's corpse bleeding into the carpet. It is a smell so gruesome as to be textured, a wet warmth webbing over this house. It lives in the clefts of scuff marks, the flower's budding parasol, under the floorboards, wedged between the dusty blades of the ceiling fan.

"Honey, I'm worried about you. This house, it isn't right. There's something wrong with the walls; it's the spirits. They're unhappy. I want to help you but honestly I don't know what more I can do."

In Haunani's last days of hospice, I said the same thing perched over her planked body, the bed soaked with perspiration, smears of urine. She was breathing so horribly, like broken fingers grasping for rope, and it's true we didn't have enough time, and it's true I was in love with her. For two decades I was in love with her but also I was in love with my son, or the idea of my son, or the daydream that once I had a son. It was easy to discard my husband, but it didn't seem fair, choosing between Haunani and my son. Such a tired cliché, like they had to hate each other, like my whole heart can only accommodate space for one. Lono forced me to choose. He forced me to choose: him or Haunani. Lono forced me because it is so much easier to think poorly of my son, this thing I made, than to think poorly of my dead wife. I can't have lost both of my own volition. I remember running my fingers up her throat as if I might energize her body into breathing properly. I remember the hours and days and the months I prepared for this loss. Is it possible to overprepare, to live the feared thing so entirely as to find it bland and diluted when it appears for good?

Anela has moved to the Ewa wall. She massages the multiplying scuff marks as one might coddle a house pet, or an egg.

"Have you ever had a ghost?" I ask her.

She snorts. "Of course I have. There are ghosts everywhere, and everyone has had at least one ghost in their life. Anyone who tells you otherwise is lying."

I don't tell her this is a ghost I would like to keep.

Anela yanks the blanket from the corpse flower and drapes it over her shoulders, her stubby little toes poking out like ten dead eyes. I wait for the corpse flower to respond, but she doesn't move. Anela says how proud she is of me, seeing me out and about. She shivers under the blanket. Says it's so cold in here, how do I stand it? Could I turn down the A/C? And bring her a cup of tea? Just the hot water and some honey and a squirt of lemon would do. The blanket feels nice. Then Anela is asleep, and I am rummaging in the hall closet for a clean linen with which to drape her so they don't have to share the one.

BUT I CAN'T sleep with Anela in the house.

I go outside. Sit in Haunani's old koa rocking chair on the back lānai because my joints are too stiff to manage sitting on the steps. The sky sweeps over us, a swath of black, blinking white stars purling through the darkness. From the lānai I can see flashes of the city. Artificial lights and the shriek of cars jutting across the highway. I'd never wanted to live so close to the city; once I was married to a man and we made our home on the dry wedge of Nānākuli and Lono had a parcel of land infested with feral chickens and stray cats where he could scrape his knees and dig through mud until he couldn't feel his fingers. The only sounds were the scuttles of cranky roosters, distant chortles from a neighbor's pig farm. Lono puckered on my lap, snoring soundly. Then came Haunani, his school's new principal. I introduced myself, and she was thrilled to meet me.

Fingering my cell phone in my pocket, I think about Lono and how improbable it is to love someone so fiercely you are willing to dismantle your son, how special and rare a love like that must be. I am a lucky woman. The corpse flower inside snuggles under the blanket. If I were to call my son right now, here is what I would say: I miss you, and I think about your happiness but not every day, and I would love to meet your child, really I would love to see you both. We could catch up, and your child could see the corpse flower. I know you didn't force me to choose, just as I know some mornings I wake up certain I made the wrong choice. I'm sorry. I know you study birds, I know everything there is to know about you.

Inside Anela has shed her blanket in favor of sharing the one I've draped over the corpse flower, and the flower's arms bend around her. Fold her like a skinned chrysalis. Now the flower has nudged a sprig of head from its neck, pale and egg-shaped. I know it's Haunani without seeing the emerald sheen burst in her eyes, her face crimped like cottage cheese and those innocuous lips. I know it's her by the way she holds Anela. I've known the whole time, so why are my hands shaking?

I stand over them. They are so old and tired. I stand over them and wait for something to happen. They're sleeping fine, it's late, and nothing happens. Why do I have only one pillow? A sofa should be dressed in decorative pillows, upholstered in tufted velvet and ribbed with tassels. To my chest I hold the lonely throw pillow, a simple beige square. So many things in this house do not belong to me, like ghosts, like love. I know I have been selfish. The guts of the pillow are firm, calloused over by gross neglect. I know. The fabric hums like chattering teeth beneath my fingers. I bring the pillow close to Anela's face, to Haunani's faceless bulb, as the first true burst of grief sprouts in my throat. They don't wake up, and I throw the pillow on the ground and water every plant in the house, the dying pīkake and lokelani rose and gardenias and the hibiscus and the orchids and ʻilima, until the floors are steeped in a muddy sludge and I've given away all my love.

THE CORPSE FLOWER starts to wilt, and the smell is something abrasive, a giant burst of decay that throttles my chest. I don't know what to compare it to. I've smelled fields of rotting fish, my wife's stale dead body lying in our bed, but this isn't that. This is a mass with legs.

Sometimes I think I am doing something brave. My roofed nursery of flowers has effloresced into something unrecognizable, a greenhouse of florals swelling in their little potted caps. Icy white petals ascend toward the ceiling, stems regenerate, leaves flash green with contentment. My indoor garden is flourishing, the scuff marks recede into the walls.

The corpse flower is dying, I think. Nothing else can explain the smell, or the way the limbs have retreated into its shell, or the unsightly wither of a once-towering spathe. Supposedly, I am lucky to see a corpse flower in full bloom for longer than twenty-four hours, but lucky is a state of mind. If I were truly lucky, I would move out of this haunted house and begin anew. I would reconcile with my son. Finally, I would tell him I am sorry.

I throw a party. Really it's a Come-See-the-Corpse-Flower-Before-I-Toss-It Party, though I tell some of my quilting friends it's my birthday. To Haunani's friends, I say it's our anniversary. I invite Lono but don't hear back. I ask Anela to bring the cake. We gather in my too-small living room and no one dares to sit on the sofa next to the dying thing because we're all too old and it might be contagious. The ladies palm their noses, talk around the smell, and when I swallow a gulp of wine, I feel something wide and permanent fracture in my chest.

"I've missed your calls, my friend," Anela says. We sit together in the kitchen on matching wood-backed chairs, sucking li hing seeds while the powder dyes our fingers.

"You'll need to come over more often. Have you seen the rest of the plants? Even your anthurium is blooming."

"And what will you do with the corpse flower?"

I lick at the dried plum, let the powder dapple my tongue in surprise. "The art museum is interested in it. You know the last hurricane season all but destroyed the garden exhibit."

"You can't give her to the museum!"

"Why not? I can't keep her here. And I already called them. Did you know this is the first corpse flower they've seen in over three decades?"

"That's exactly why she should stay here with you!"

"It's taking up too much space. I already have *so many* plants."

"Then throw them out! Or give the corpse flower to me. You can give her to me." Anela has never raised her voice at me like this. It's an empowering feeling, to know I can still so fluently coax rage from the other woman. I stare at her as if she's gone mad.

"Why would I do a crazy thing like that?"

WHEN THE NEW corpse flower exhibit launches at the Honolulu Museum of Art, I attend the opening show alone. I wear the same slate-black wrap dress I wore once to Haunani's wake and I carry a flask in my leather clutch corking the same dry gin. Supposedly, as the benefactor, I am this evening's guest of honor, though the only indication of such reverence is an annual membership to the museum and a complimentary decorative scarf. I am also invited to browse the open bar at my leisure.

The museum lives on the foothills of Ward Avenue, tucked into paving-stoned walls and a wide, pitched roof. If you were to ask after its origins, volunteer docents would spin tales of flagstones cut from Molokaʻi granite, Hawaiian lava rock filched from the hills of Kaimukī. I wander the courtyard and stand beneath a coral arch. I can't hold my alcohol the way I used to, and all the gin sops my stomach like an old sponge. The exhibit's curators are lively women washed in moonlight and shimmers of white wine. They want to know where the flower came from, how on earth I'd managed to nurse a multi-week blooming cycle, how I could ever live with such a smell in my house. I try my best to answer their questions, and when I extend my hand for a smoked ahi canapé, I crane my neck around the room, terrified I might find Anela blinking at me through the crowd.

I find the garden. Guests usher through the winding cobbled path, wineglasses clutched between drunk fingers. Docents pass out complimentary facemasks, should the smell trigger an intolerable disgust. They wade through an ocean of ivy, clusters of ʻamaʻu ferns, and burgeoning yellow shower trees and emerge to face the wilting corpse flower, its ivory spadix folded toward the dirt as the flower slips into dormancy. The guests curl fingers over their noses, shove away the wretched smell. Some speak of Limburger cheese; others declare the odor akin to a cat's litterbox neglected for months. Sadness roils inside me like clumped aluminum. How badly I wish these strangers could've seen her in her prime, when her spire soared well over five feet and I draped her aging limbs with a clean, pressed sheet. I wish this so badly the bowl of my wineglass splinters in my hand. Shards pierce the softened pad of my palm. Glass washes the ground in winks of bright light. People gather around me, commanding loudly, ushering me away from all the shards, but they cannot feel the strength of my fingers as I clench a single waxen wedge of glass in my fist, clench it until I can't see the corpse flower clearly anymore. Until I open my eyes and see the two arms, two legs, the truncated neck and the featureless orb of my lover's face pressing into my clouded sight. Blood swims down my hand in ribbons.

It will take many months for the corpse flower to die, while this bleeding will quickly be attended to. I will drop the glass shard and let the docents clean and bandage me. I will go home, alone alone alone, ad nauseam. For now, though, I am the gallery's centerpiece. I sink into all the eyes pressing against me, and breathe anew.

ACKNOWLEDGMENTS

This book owes the entirety of its life to the people who have shaped me, inspired me, made me. To my kūpuna and ancestors who came before—thank you. I hope this work makes you proud and does justice to our stories.

Iwalani Kim believed in these stories even before I could cultivate belief. She is my fiercest advocate and a beautiful friend, and I'm so grateful to have her by my side through publication and beyond. Proud to be forever president of the Iwalani Fan Club. And to everyone at Sanford J. Greenburger Associates, especially Maddie Wallace—thank you so much for your enduring support.

Callie Garnett approached these stories with enthusiasm, rigor, and an intrinsic understanding of my intentions, a beautiful alchemy that enabled this collection to arrive at its current form. I will forever be thankful for our partnership. And to the Bloomsbury team, Team Every Drop—I am so grateful for everyone who has nurtured this book to publication, especially Jillian Ramirez, Akshaya Iyer, Ben Chisnall, Lauren Moseley, Katie Vaughn, Rosie Mahorter, Emily Fishman, Patti Ratchford, Jaya Miceli (who designed a cover so gorgeous I'm still gasping at it), Geo Willis, Tom Skipp, Jo Forshaw, Emma Stephenson, and Alona Fryman.

Thank you to the incredibly talented writers who have so generously supported this collection: Elizabeth McCracken, Amy Hempel, T Kira Māhealani Madden, Joseph Han, Molly Antopol, Kimberly King Parsons, Laura van den Berg, Kali Fajardo-Anstine, Jenny Tinghui Zhang, Marisa Crane, Helen Phillips, and Hilma

ACKNOWLEDGMENTS

Wolitzer. I admire you all, and still can't believe how lucky I am to be read by you.

Thank you to the editors who were the first champions of these stories, including Kathryn Draney, Amy Hempel, Lou Ann Walker, Maria Kuznetsova, Thomas Renjilian, and Kaush Suresh.

To the brilliant and supportive instructor and writers with whom I worked at Tin House, including Kimberly King Parsons, Andrea Bishop, Jinwoo Chong, Camille Jacobson, Reena Shah, Timea Sipos, April Sopkin, and Tanya Žilinskas, thank you for encountering my work with equal parts enthusiasm and rigor. And to my instructor and fellow writers at the Bread Loaf Writers' Conference, including Laura van den Berg, Mac Crane, Dana Liebelson, Zach Powers, David Schwartz, and Pallavi Wakharkar, thank you for your insights that made my work stronger and more itself.

To my community at the Michener Center for Writers and the New Writers Project—I know without question this book would not exist without your companionship, advice, and support. Thank you to my loves Stephanie Macias Gibson, Brynne Jones, Luci Arbus-Scandiffio, Bradley Trumpfheller, Kyle Francis Williams, Reena Shah, Molly Williams, Carrie R. Moore, Felipe Bomeny, Justin Bui, Amanda Bestor-Siegal, Ellaree Yeagley, Bev Chukwu, Karl-Mary Akre, Maryan Nagy Captan, Alejandro Puyana, Rickey Fayne, Colwill Brown, Juan Fernando Villagómez, Zack Schlosberg, Sophia Emmons-Bell, Gracie Newman, Eileen Chong, and Laurel Faye. And a special thank you to the mentors, instructors, and administrators who made my time at the Michener Center so extraordinary, including Bret Anthony Johnston, Elizabeth McCracken, Molly Antopol, Edward Carey, Amy Hempel, Deb Olin Unferth, Maya Perez, Sarah Matthes, Lisa Olstein, Mitchell S. Jackson, Nathan Patton, Charles Ramírez Berg, Heather Houser, Holly Doyel, Blake Lee Pate, and Billy Fatzinger.

ACKNOWLEDGMENTS

Thank you to my friends, from home and from beyond, for sustaining belief in me whenever my own belief waned. Love you forever Kaylin Tsukayama, Manuokalani Tupper, Meaghan Tomas, Jairus Kiyonaga, Raelin Perez, Alexander Steele, Josh Prickel, Amy Ren, Kylie Yamauchi, Megan Yamauchi, Natalie Garcia, Tom Iwanicki, Shreya Yadav, Claire Lewis, and Sarah Yamanaka.

To Kyle Nakatsuka, for his meticulous attention to the language and ʻŌlelo Hawaiʻi transcribed in these stories.

To my community at Kamehameha Schools, and to the teachers who first inspired me to take writing seriously, including Wendie Burbridge, Lionel Barona, Sarah Razee, Stephanie Darrow, Shari Chan, Diana Fontaine, and Jim Slagel. And especially to Princess Bernice Pauahi Bishop, I remain forever indebted to you.

Thank you to my family, who has never questioned my love for books, for writing, and for perpetually staying in school. To my parents, to whom this book is dedicated, thank you. I will never know how I got so lucky as to be taught how to live thoughtfully and responsibly in this world by you both. Thank you to my sister Noelle Kakimoto, to grams and papa, to grandma and grandpa, and to the rest of our wide and wonderful ʻohana. I truly would not be where I am today without your unwavering love and support.

Finally, thank you to my forever love Van Wishingrad, who reminded me how cool it is to be a writer on our very first date. Two pets and many moves later, and you're still my most favorite person.

A NOTE ON THE AUTHOR

MEGAN KAMALEI KAKIMOTO is a Japanese and Kanaka Maoli (native Hawaiian) writer from Honolulu, Hawaiʻi. Her fiction has been featured in *Granta*, *Conjunctions*, *Joyland*, and elsewhere. She has been a finalist for the Keene Prize for Literature and has received support from the Rona Jaffe Foundation and the Bread Loaf Writers' Conference. She received her MFA from the Michener Center for Writers, where she was a Fiction Fellow. She lives in Honolulu.